HELL BENT

CALISTA LYNNE

AMBLE
PRESS
ANN ARBOR

2022

For my beloved friends and enemies.

When I said I was skipping rehearsal to write,
I was actually in Times Square buying a latex dress.

Sorry.

CHAPTER ONE

In which a demon is summoned and milkshakes never arrive.

Dear Marcus,
I forgive you.
There isn't anything the tabloids or the news can say that will change my mind.

See you soon,
Julia R. Tolliver

Asbury Park is in mourning, just like me.

The summer breeze and the calm ocean are gloomy at three in the morning beneath a New Jersey pier. Well, not a pier, exactly. I'm under the Paramount Theatre, which is held above the sand by metal beams that have probably seen more dirty deals than any back alley in the city. I expected there to be other people here—stoners or the homeless—but there's no one. Just me, five Bahama Breeze-scented Yankee Candles, and a pentagram drawn in the sand. I wish I could say this is out of character, but I constantly seem to end up in indecent, and occasionally immoral, situations. No, I've never attempted this

1

before, but seventeen years of ignored "Do Not Enter" signs and obsessive tendencies doesn't make what I'm currently attempting that much of a stretch.

The wind catches a *BuzzFeed* article I printed out earlier today, *How to Summon and Bind a Demon This Halloween.* It flutters out of reach and lands directly on a candle.

"Shit." I kick sand on the tiny flames, resulting in two more candles going out and a corner of the pentagram smudging.

"Shit. Shit. Shit."

Picking up the article, I note that a few steps have been burnt off, and am suddenly grateful to live in a world with unlimited data. I pull my phone out from my bra and wait a frankly egregious amount of time for *BuzzFeed* to load without Wi-Fi. No one said how difficult this demon summoning business would be, but who would? I only have one friend and as much as I like to believe she would support what I'm doing, even I realize this scheme is hard to get behind.

Jules, I imagine Laura chastising me, *he's only a guy. Get over it.*

He isn't just a guy, though. Marcus *is* the world.

Anyway, Laura has slowly been transforming into something she refers to as "mature," meaning less talk of Marcus and more talk of studying. Soon she's going to start using awful phrases like "kids these days" and "back in my day." In my opinion, it's not so much being "mature" as being "boring."

As the article loads, I hunt down a stick to fix the corner of the pentagram, then go around re-lighting all of the candles for what feels like the hundredth time. The breeze is nice, but ultimately unhelpful.

Eventually the *BuzzFeed* logo pops up and I scroll down to the next step, which is to pour virgin blood on the pentagram. It says that tomato juice is an acceptable substitute, but I decide to go for the real deal. It's a good thing Marcus is the only man I've ever had eyes for and that he's more than twice my age, British, and trapped on the other side of a television screen. I pull a switchblade out of my pocket and press the button, watching the blade spring out with an uneasy sort of excitement. A year or so ago, I went to one of those nerd conventions—my alternative to church—and bought a pink spring-loaded pocket knife from a metalsmith who made fandom-inspired weapons. Owning a knife is cool. Calling it a switchblade is doubly cool.

Before the candles can go out again, I drag the blade across my thigh, slicing it open far enough beneath my white shorts that the blood won't stain. *Motherfucker,* I think, dropping the knife into the sand immediately and gasping in a totally unattractive way, *that stings.*

Focus. Focus. This scar is going to look so cool one day.

If this is truly what it takes to bind a demon to me and make sure he can't run away, it'll be worth it.

Right?

But the blood is crawling in a morbid path down my leg and I wonder if this is a step too far. This is real. This is me declaring that I actually think I can do this.

Deep breaths. The stinging continues and blood drips down to my socks. I refocus and rub my hand all over my thigh, spreading red around in large circles over my skin, then move to press crimson handprints into the sand. More blood falls, seeping steadily around where I walk. More than I had originally anticipated.

Surely that can only help the process.

Surely.

But damn it burns.

The waves lap gently at the shore. I scramble back to my phone only to find that touch ID does not work when your hands are covered in bodily fluids and grit. *Huh.* I clumsily type in the passcode (Marcus' birthday) with my left hand, smudging the screen, and kneel down. Some of the sand gets blown into my cut.

Another candle flickers out.

"*Shit!*"

I relight it with my bloody hand while holding the phone in the other, consulting the article for my final step. The Latin I'm

3

meant to chant isn't written out phonetically, but I'm sure it's the intention that counts. I give it a go in the most theatrical voice I can muster.

"*Praecipio tibi coram me* . . ." I trail off when the screen dims, and leave another fingerprint behind when I tap it. "*Moloch! Praecipio tibi coram me Moloch et reuerterunt.*"

I wait a few moments in heavy silence, toss my phone into the sand, then tack on a "Please."

Everything inside me is vibrating. The world shouldn't be so calm right now, but the ocean is as still as I've ever seen it. The unnatural scent of the candles fills the air.

No birds cry out. Nothing. Everything is serene.

Until it isn't.

Darkness, total darkness, passes in front of my eyes. Not merely an absence of light, but like it never existed to begin with. An endless void that is everywhere and everything.

The sound of heavy breathing breaks through the Nothing. Agonized and exhausted gasps in the dark.

And as quickly as it came on, the blackness lifts.

My eyes actually have to readjust to the brightness of the night. I place a hand on my chest, as if to double-check that all of me is still present and accounted for, when my brain catches up to my eyes and I see what's right in front of me: a man sprawled out in the center of my pentagram.

Blinking in astonishment, I take him in for a few moments, while he does exactly the same back at me.

Then I scream.

"Who the hell are you?" I shout, holding up my arms as if to say *stay back*.

His eyes dart around as he slowly gets to his feet, looking slightly rumpled and more than a little shocked. He brushes the sand off of his outfit. A yellow button up and grey skinny jeans.

It would appear that I accidentally summoned a twink. One who looks vaguely like a younger, impeccably groomed John Legend.

"That's a bit of a rude greeting, wouldn't you say?" he asks, and I swear I recognize his voice from somewhere. "You're the one who summoned me."

I squint at him. Are those ... margaritas on his shirt?

"You're Moloch?" I ask, disbelievingly. Where are the wings? The horns? The cloven hooves and red skin? The most demonic thing about this guy is the fact that his haircut looks like he tripped into someone holding electric clippers.

"No, I'm not. But I am the next best thing. Or, at least," he gestures to the Yankee Candles and raises an eyebrow, "the best thing you had any chance of summoning with all this."

"So, you're not Moloch, but you are a demon?" I cross my arms.

"Indeed I am. The genuine article."

He trails off for a second, and I try to come to terms with the fact that this is not a television show or a movie, but real life, and I am actually in New Jersey and that is actually a real live demon.

Is *live* even the correct word?

"Now as much as I love hanging out with you, why don't you break this pentagram and let me go?" he says. "Busy man, me. Got some curses to cast and people to poke with a pitchfork."

"You don't look like a demon."

"And you don't look like a Satanist. Appearances can be deceptive."

"I'm not a Satanist," I say.

"Even better. Then you won't mind smudging out a little corner of this pentagram and letting me go."

"Sorry, no can do. I need your help."

"You don't want it," he shoots back. His voice echoes faintly through the air around us, his words being carried out to sea.

"I know what I want."

I try not to become heated. People think I don't really want to be a lawyer, that I just want to argue. They think that when I say Marcus K. Dixon saved my life, I'm exaggerating. But if there's one thing I know, it's my own mind.

The demon raises a hand placatingly.

5

"Calm down. What's gotten your panties in such a twist? Boyfriend troubles? Girlfriend troubles? Friend troubles? Troubles?" He plops back down in the sand, sitting cross-legged and slouched, the epitome of *done*. "You *do* realize I live in Hell, right? I'm probably not the most helpful."

Deep breaths. This is normal. This is fine. This is New Jersey.

"The reason I need you is because you live in Hell." I work through the words slowly, thinking about them one at a time as I look down into the sand. I hadn't expected to get this far. "I need you to take me there."

He laughs. It's a broken sound.

"Oh, wow. I thought you might be misguided or something. But no! You really are an idiot."

"And what does that make you?"

He shrugs.

"I guess that makes me someone stupid enough to get captured by an idiot. Tell me, what business do you have in Hell?"

"Someone important died. I need to bring him back."

Saying it out loud makes me realize how absolutely insane this entire plan is. This is why you should never mix tequila stolen from your parents, sadness, and Wikipedia holes. One moment you're marathoning the complete filmography of the only man you'll ever love, the next you're researching ways to bring him back from the dead. Just teenage girl things.

I wish I was drunk now and not sober enough to realize how completely insane this all is.

"That's probably the worst answer you could have given me. Nope. You are not going to Hell."

Fine. This is why I considered a few options before choosing which way to summon a demon. I say nothing, just stick out my foot and dig it into a point of the pentagram. The demon tips a make-believe hat, stands, makes a grand gesture with his arms, then looks rather surprised when nothing happens. Attempting to school his expression, he straightens out his shirt and begins to walk away. He gets to the edge of the pier before letting out a scream—not a melodramatic one like in the movies, but small and whimpering—and falls to his knees. I don't let it affect me.

"You alright there?" I ask, slowly walking towards him.

"What did you do?" he seethes from between clenched teeth.

"If *BuzzFeed* was correct, and *BuzzFeed* usually is, I haven't just summoned you. You're bound to me."

He looks at me with an expression of nearly deranged terror; his dark eyes rove my body searchingly before stopping on my thigh. Suddenly, he is up and wriggling extremely tight skinny jeans down to his knees. Before I can express how desperately I want him *not to do that*, he points to a silver scar on the side of his thigh and sputters.

"What. The. Hell. Did. You. Do?" He finally spits out. I move closer and appraise the mark.

"Wow," I say. "We match." I point to my own wound, jagged, sandy, bleeding sluggishly.

"Do you know what this means?" he asks, grabbing me by my shoulders.

"What the hell? Let me go."

He holds on tighter and it hurts; fingers dig in and surely leave marks. I try to yank my arm away but he only tightens his grip.

"We're stuck together," he tells me, eyes manic. "If I get too far away from you it'll cause me agonizing pain! I've heard the horror stories about binding, we all have. Why did you even think doing something like that would be a good idea?"

"Because I want you to take me to Hell."

"I am a demon," he says, coldly, looking me dead in the eye even though he's a full head taller than me. "Can you comprehend that? Do you understand the consequences of what you have done?"

"Let me go." An ironic request, considering the situation.

He releases my arm slowly and I don't say anything else, trying to convey that I am not buying into his bad boy routine, regardless of the fact that he probably is a very bad boy indeed.

"Where did you find those instructions again?" he asks, pulling up his pants.

"*BuzzFeed.*"

"You'll have to tell me more about it. We'll have the time, considering I won't be able to let you out of my sight. Don't you want any privacy?"

I shrug. I've never had enough friends to make lack of privacy a major concern, and I don't mind if Laura knows everything about me. I want to know everything about her. Privacy seems a bit abstract. The demon kicks the sand in frustration.

"I never should have come here," he says to the ocean.

"I thought you didn't have a choice, what with me summoning you and all that."

"Sure," he says flatly, looking very much like a man who has given up.

"Now bring me to Hell."

"Okay, look—"

"Hey, what are you two doing over there?" a gruff voice interrupts, shouting from farther down the beach. Moments later a light is pointed in our direction. I see someone who might be an old widower out for a 3 a.m. stroll or more likely, security approaching us.

"Oh no," I whisper urgently. "We gotta go."

"What?"

"We probably shouldn't be here right now," I say, thinking, *and this is not how you spend your last summer before getting an anthropology degree.*

"I'm not moving. Not until we work out how you're going to release me from whatever binding nonsense you pulled."

"Fine," I say, grabbing my knife and shoving it into my pocket. I sprint in the opposite direction of the man with the flashlight, my shoes sinking into the sand with each step. Say what you will about cute white short shorts and butter yellow crop tops, but they definitely don't hold you back when there's a lot of running to do. A disgruntled sort of groan comes from behind me and I know my new demonic partner is rushing to catch up.

I want to feel bad about the fact that if he didn't follow me, he'd suffer bodily pain, but he *is* a demon. I dash past more metal pillars holding up the theater, not trying overly hard to avoid the broken glass and shells that litter the sand, until I am out from beneath the building and the sky is stretched out, dark and clouded, above. I reach the ramp to the boardwalk unscathed and run up it and off of the beach as quickly as I can.

There's no way the demon and I don't look suspicious now, but I still hope the old man isn't in pursuit as I cross the boards in a hurry. They creak unforgivingly beneath my feet. I veer to the right and down the steps to Ocean Avenue, towards my poorly—and illegally—parallel-parked Chevy Spark.

Graffiti and faded signs flash by as I dart across the street, reaching the vehicle in seconds. Thankfully, the doors don't need to be unlocked; doing so encourages the alarm to go off more frequently so I never bother locking them to begin with. I scramble in and toss the switchblade blindly into the passenger seat.

"What are you running for?" I hear the twink—I really need to get his name—shout as he catches up and opens the back door, diving in head first. I ignore him and pull out of the parking space. We're off. The painting of Tillie's grotesquely smiling face bares his teeth at us as we speed past the Wonder Bar, then a truly unnecessary number of stop signs. I turn to the right and drive until there are more houses than empty gift shops on either side of the road.

The fluorescent lights of suburbia blow past us and Not-Moloch sits up in the backseat.

"How do we get to Hell?" I ask, heading towards the Garden State Parkway. I need a road I can think on. Somewhere to plan.

"We don't. You unbind me and I go back to Hell alone to wallow in the indignity of it all."

"Sorry, not gonna happen. I need to go to Hell and you're going to take me."

"What could you possibly need in the afterlife? I thought you brought me here to, I don't know, kill someone. Or play a few pranks." He changes tone, all calm reason now. "This is

9

all happening very quickly, maybe we should sit down and talk things over."

I ignore him for the time being. There's too much to explain and I don't even understand half of what I'm doing myself.

Right before getting on the entrance ramp, I notice a poster for the Jersey Shore Roller Girls hanging on the side of a building to the left. Oh, to be in a roller derby league. That's probably a better way of dealing with one's emotions than whatever I just did. Maybe once this is all over, I'll take up strapping wheels to my feet and pummeling other women for fun.

Stop.

Daydreaming may be my favorite pastime, but now is not an opportune moment. I redirect my thoughts to my current reality, even if it is completely unhinged. The parkway is nice and empty at this time of the night, only the occasional truck passing by. I go slower than I usually would in order to give us time to talk.

"Someone died and I need him back. The entire world does," I explain again.

"Who?"

I glance at the demon and make the executive decision that this card is probably best kept close to my chest for the time being. At least until we properly get the ball rolling.

"I'm not telling you until we get there."

"How are you so sure he's in Hell?" he asks.

"I wasn't until you showed up and proved that Hell actually exists."

"Yeah, but maybe he went to Heaven. You know, like someone decent enough to be worth saving would have?"

"No. He didn't."

We sit in silence for a hot second, me trying to mask my gut-dropping terror as excitement. I never expected to get this far; typically, my dumbass schemes start out amazing and slowly fizzle into disappointing resolutions. Take the time I stole Mom's car to attend a film premiere in Manhattan and ended up stranded on the side of the road with an empty gas tank instead. She didn't punish me; I'm not certain she would even know how to, but it goes to prove that I have the greatest dreams and the most ineffective means of executing them.

I pretend to be a character in some grand, sweeping melodrama and put on a brave face.

"I'm only going to ask you one more time. Take me to Hell."

"No."

"Then tell me how to get there myself."

"You can't. I have to create an entryway and a human definitely wouldn't survive going through that alone. Not to mention I'm not really sure about the extent of my bound-up powers. Thanks for that, by the way."

Just my luck.

"Okay. Fine."

I exit the parkway. We're in some tiny town with weirdly nice houses, which makes me wonder why someone who obviously has money to burn would choose New Jersey as the furnace. It doesn't take much driving around in the dark to come across one of the cornerstones of our society: the strip mall. I pull the car into the parking lot, staying a good distance away from the building, but keep the front of the car pointed at it. I turn to Not-Moloch in the backseat, who looks slightly worse for wear despite the cocky smile he's sporting.

I have an idea, a horrible one, but an idea, nonetheless. I weigh bound powers and a reluctant demon against my desire to save Marcus and am not completely surprised by the result.

"Can you open an entryway to Hell on demand or is it a whole sort of process?"

"I don't see how that's any of your business."

"Fine."

I face forward, put the car back in drive, and press on the gas. No thoughts.

"Watch out," he warns casually, obviously not taking any of this as deadly serious as he damn well should. I ignore him, stare straight ahead, and go faster.

No thoughts.

I'm not scared of much, especially not death. Not when I

have something to prove. I'm never scared of death.

"Um, there's a wall right there," he tries, starting to realize I'm not playing around. The side of the building gets closer and closer. My heart has never beaten so fast in all my life, and I imagine whatever is making my brain all fuzzy must be adrenaline. There's a bitter taste at the back of my throat. I smile, and prepare to ram into the brick wall and, you know, death.

But we don't hit a wall.

There is the whizzbang of firecrackers and a flurry of neon. Out the front windshield is an explosion of colors, all splattered and bright, swirling around like oil on water. It's like nothing I've ever seen before, and I barely have time to blink, to seal the image behind my eyelids, when the maddening vortex gives way to another parking lot. It's a different one, as if we'd never been driving towards a building at all.

"*Brake! Brake! Brake!*" Not-Moloch yells, and without thinking, I slam my foot down on the brakes. We scream together and swerve towards a building. My brain is nowhere near functional enough to figure out what's going on. I spin the wheel to the left, dragging it hand over hand as far as it can go as we skid to a stop mere inches from something that is most certainly not a strip mall.

We've gone somewhere else. Somewhere entirely new.

"Is this a joke to you?" he asks, nearly climbing into the front seat and spitting with rage. "You bound my powers, you colossal idiot, and entryways aren't the easiest thing to make happen in normal circumstances."

I shrug, feeling spectacularly unaffected by that brush with death. If I were an intellectual, I'd say it's on account of desensitization due to time spent in a hospital and watching violent films starring the love of my life. Sadly, though, I am not an intellectual and just don't have a firm enough grasp on what death is to think it's that scary.

Obviously.

"Where are we?"

"Where do you think? Hell. Congratulations, you got what

you wanted." He throws his hands up, narrowly missing my face. "Now what possessed you to do something as stupid as that? You could have died!"

Another shrug. I stare into my lap. "Either you'd do exactly this, or I'd die and achieve the same result. Entry into Hell."

He snorts and leans into the backseat, trying to appear less frantic.

"Charming to hear you're anticipating an eternity of punishment after you die."

Beyond the windshield is a dull, beige sky—like something out of a sepia tone photograph—stretched out above a crappy diner we almost ran into. Everything is normal to the point that it's creepy. Picture book illustrations and movie sets are this ordinary, not reality. This feels plastic, with all the colors shining a bit too bright.

"Are you sure we aren't still in New Jersey?" I ask.

"Close, but no. This is Purgatory."

"I thought you said we were in Hell."

"Purgatory is a region of Hell. You were impressively unspecific with your request."

He sighs, and I can practically hear the thoughts whizzing around inside his head. It feels like he's starting to give in. Just a little bit. Just enough for me to begin convincing him that I'm braver than I am stupid, and what I have planned is an expression of that bravery.

"Why don't we go inside and have a discussion like two civilized people?" he finally asks.

"We're not people. You're a demon and I'm a teenager. There's a difference between us and 'people.'"

Still, I open up the door and get out. The air in Hell feels thicker than it did on Earth, and it smells of cheesesteaks. My demon companion gets out and leads me up concrete steps to the entrance. He pushes the door open and inside, my eyes are met with rows of booths and a line of cherry-red stools at a gleaming chrome counter. There are many people seated around the place, some in small groupings and others all alone, but no one looks particularly demonic or evil.

Not-Moloch walks in like he owns the place, and I follow close behind, trying not to be obvious as I peek at tables full of the most unexpected pairings. People are playing cards and staring at walls. Lying face down in the booths. We sit on stools covered in cheap vinyl directly in front of the window that looks into the kitchen. Steam pours out. I start to feel duped because we are almost certainly still in New Jersey; nothing about this place is hellish in the slightest.

Not-Moloch looks everywhere but at me, craning his neck as if he's hunting for something. Swiveling around, he evidently finds it.

"Shax!" he shouts, waving his arms without an ounce of self-consciousness. "I'm back." Turning to see what he's looking at, I spot a woman in a mint green dress. Clichéd fifties style, like everything else, but her face is carved by deep wrinkles. She looks like she's never even heard of happiness, let alone experienced it. She walks towards us from a booth against the wall, her black leather shoes clacking against the linoleum floor.

"What are you doing back here already?" she says in a stern voice, moving to stand on the other side of the counter. He gestures to himself as if to say, *Who, me?* Her frown deepens in response, creating even more wrinkles.

"I finally got rid of you and you come back to harass me almost immediately." She grabs a disgusting-looking cloth from underneath the counter and begins wiping down glasses, leaving behind streaks of dirt and grime. "Do your job," she says to my demon companion.

"Shax, you always say the sweetest things. I *am* doing my job. I think. I'm definitely doing something moderately demonic."

He shoots me a smile, full of teeth but clearly lacking genuine happiness. Shax shakes her head and disappears through a door. It creaks as it swings back and forth.

And back and forth. And back and forth.

"Bring us two strawberry milkshakes while you're in there," he shouts, obviously too late for the woman to hear him. I look down and catch my reflection on the counter, distorted and grim. The kitchen door keeps swinging in time with music coming from a jukebox hiding in the corner.

Shifty Henry said to Bugs, 'For heaven's sake
No one's looking now's the chance to make a break.'

Distorted and grim.

"Tell me," Not-Moloch says, smacking his hands on the table and turning to me, "what's a nice young lady like yourself doing in a Godforsaken place like this? Or, more precisely, why the actual fuck would you summon a demon to bring you here?"

I do intend to answer his question, but first I ask, "What's your name?"

Creaking doors. Elvis croons.

"How about this," he tries. "If you answer my question, I'll answer yours."

"Sure. I summoned you because I need your help."

"Yes. We covered that. You want to bring someone back from the dead. Oh no, this really is a boy problem thing, isn't it?"

"No! Don't be so sexist," I say, faux-scandalized. "Marcus isn't a boy, he's a man."

If looks could kill, I'd . . . well, I'd probably be in exactly the same place.

"You knew a man so awful you're certain he has ended up in the boiling, sulfurous, agonizing pits of Hell and you decided to come down here yourself and drag him out? And you're gonna say you don't have boy problems? That's idiocy."

"That's love."

He's silent, looking at me like I'm even more stupid than he previously thought, an expression I am well acquainted with.

"It's love, is it? Well, that changes everything. And please, tell me, would this guy walk willingly into Hell for you, or would he leave you here for an eternity of torment and sobriety?"

I consider lying but the truth will come out eventually. Might as well explain it now and save myself the shame later. I swivel around on the stool, intermittently kicking my feet against the pedestal, and say, "No. He wouldn't. He doesn't know I exist."

"Literally or metaphorically?"

"Literally." I mentally prepare to never be cool again. "Let me lay it out for you: the person you are going to help me rescue is a forty-three-year-old actor. His name is Marcus K. Dixon. British. Plays Fletcher Fatale, my favorite superhero. Unbelievably attractive. Amazingly kind. Has fantastic chemistry with his co-star, Percy Whithorn, who plays his nemesis, Ferdinand Ferdinand—"

"Ferdinand Ferdinand?"

"It's not important. Two weeks ago, Marcus was found dead in a hotel room in Italy surrounded by heroin and hookers. Which is what leads me to believe there's a good chance he's in Hell right now."

"Hey, you're being unfair to heroin and hookers—"

"Let me finish." I hold up my hand for silence so I can continue my somewhat preplanned spiel. "He also has a daughter. Her name is Elle Dixon and she's my second favorite person after him. She recently graduated college and has been doing all sorts of weird crap. Last year she made a podcast called *Rich Bitch On the Run* that I'm obsessed with."

"Sounds like someone used Daddy's money to make it big."

"Shut up. She's devastated, and having to deal with her sadness all over my social media is almost as upsetting as the fact that Marcus is actually gone. You need to take me to him, wherever he's being kept, and let me bring him back to Earth."

"There is so much wrong with this plan that I don't even know where to begin." He reaches to the wire basket of condiments in front of us and begins pulling out sugar substitute packets. Sickeningly pink. "First off, doing this doesn't guarantee he will love you. He's, what, twenty years older than you?"

"Twenty-six. But he doesn't need to love me. He needs to be alive."

Except he *will* love me because that's how these things work.

"Sure. Whatever. That's the next problem. People don't come back from the dead, and little girls definitely don't drag superstars back from Hell." He begins stacking the sugar packets and constructing what appears to be a tiny house. "Don't you think that would have happened by now? Humans would notice if dead people began popping up out of their graves like, 'Hey! Was having a truly great time being tortured by my main squeeze Beelzebub but someone really wanted me to make a sequel to my last superhero movie and I thought it might be a good idea to stop decomposing and start doing that instead!'"

"I mean, Jesus did, didn't he?" I offer, pointedly ignoring his mockery.

"I'm not going to dignify that with a response."

"Dignify this with a response then: you're going to help me find him because I will not unbind you until you do. I'll leave you here, go outside, and drive away so quickly you won't be able to catch me before the excruciating pain traps you here."

"Damn. You're sadistic. I thought seventeen-year-old girls were supposed to be sweet."

"You've obviously never met one before."

I pull a sweetener packet out from the bottom of the stack and his house comes toppling down. Packets slide across the counter. He sighs.

"Did you even think past summoning me? How are you going to free this guy? Or get out of Hell? Your plan completely overlooks the fact that you will be utterly helpless and trapped in Hell forever if you lose me along the way. I hope you realize that even if I do bring you to this asshole, there is no universe where I can give you any advice on what to do after that. You'll both still be trapped here."

But we'll be trapped together.

"That's fine. I'll figure it out when I get there. Marcus is really clever; I'm sure he'll have ideas. This can be a symbiotic sort of thing: I stick with you so you don't feel debilitating pain, you stick with me so I don't end up wandering through Hell for the rest of eternity. Think it over. And while you're thinking, why don't you tell me your name?"

Honestly, it's not the question I'm most worried about right now, but it's a lot easier to ask it than figure out what I'm going to do once I get to Marcus. Thinking up this scheme in a drunken haze without knowing enough about religion to begin strategizing past the whole Moloch thing really seems to be backfiring now. But isn't that what being a teenager is all about? Doing stupid, reckless crap that you can turn into an amusing anecdote to tell over cocktails one day? You know, adult stuff. Not-Moloch looks me over assessingly.

"You can do a whole lot of damage with a demon's name. But I suppose you've already done it, haven't you? Fine. My name is Ashmodai."

"Ashmodai," I repeat, feeling out the unfamiliar syllables. "I was trying to summon Moloch. Why'd you show up instead?"

A shrug. Aspiring to be a lawyer has given me practice understanding people, and he's definitely hiding something.

"Luck of the draw, I suppose. How fortunate for me."

"Jailhouse Rock" begins again. I discreetly glance around to see if Elvis is hanging around here for some reason. I don't spot any long-dead rock stars, but there is a man two seats down with the bushiest beard I've ever seen, looking bored out of his mind. In fact, everyone looks incredibly bored. No one has any food. There isn't even a nice glass display case full of beautiful cakes and pies. No register at the front with a little bowl of mints. Still, where we are is unmistakable.

"Why does Purgatory look like a diner?" I ask.

"Why do diners look like Purgatory?" he responds. *Touché*.

Shax exits the kitchen, without strawberry milkshakes or anything else that would imply she actually does a job here. Ashmodai and I stare at one another, playing a silent game of chicken. I'm not asking for much, especially not if demons are as powerful as I've been led to believe by YouTube. Even bound, having him gets me that much closer to the reality of saving Marcus.

Of making Elle happy again.

That's the most important thing in the universe. I don't matter. Not really, not in the grand scheme of things, but Elle *does*. She isn't afraid of anything, not of being alone or the future.

18

Isn't that wonderful? Doesn't someone like that deserve to be happy? And don't I deserve to be the one who makes her happy?

"Look, you have to take me to him. Marcus is everything. Not only to me, but to so many people. And if you want to make it demonic, then fine. Tell yourself that he makes shallow, self-centered movies that glorify violence and encourage people to spend money on something with no real value. That movies are a plague on society and the ones Marcus stars in have no merit, so you're actually contributing to the dumbing down of humanity. Tell yourself whatever you need to, and I'll agree with you, but take me to him."

Ashmodai looks at me, and I get the sense that he's seeing more than just my face. I break out the most pleading puppy dog eyes I can manage.

"Shax," he calls out after a few moments, eyes not leaving me. "You've been around here a lot longer than I have. Tell me, how do I go about locating a specific human being in Hell?"

I suppress my victory wiggle.

"What are you up to?" she asks suspiciously.

"Important business. Demonic work and all that."

"Never too late to start, is it?"

He turns and flashes her a million-dollar, nine-out-of-ten-dentists-agree smile. Shax comes closer and starts picking up the sugar substitute and returning it to the little basket.

"You're looking for a human, you say? As in, someone who was on Earth and is now a resident down here?"

"Exactly that."

"You know me, Ash. I've been trapped here since Alexander the Great was straight. I'm out of touch. Besides, we both got the same knowledge dump welcome package. I'm sure you know as much as I do. You'd be better off asking The Fates."

"The Fates?" he groans. "Aren't they all the way in Drizzlyland?"

She throws a packet at his head. It almost sounds like Elvis is laughing from the speakers.

"Be grateful they aren't farther. You want advice? There's my

19

advice. Ask The Fates. There ain't nothing they don't know."

"We both know that isn't true. Seeing all potential outcomes is about as good as seeing none of them. If they really knew everything, they'd probably understand basic decency and start acting less horrible."

She gives him a stern look. Ashmodai grumbles and grabs my hand. "Come on, Jules. We weren't ever going to get those milkshakes, anyway."

"You know my name?" I ask as he drags me past bedraggled patrons and out the door. The look he gives me makes me feel so moronic I don't ask again. Demons probably know everyone's name; Shax said something about a knowledge dump. We walk to the car and I keep telling myself *This is Hell. This is Hell,* in the hope that it'll sink in. *Nothing will ever be the same again.*

This feels like the world I know, except slightly askew. Like an off-brand version of being alive. But the ground is solid beneath my feet and there's a road in the distance, and trees beyond that. If only Marcus could have ended up in that diner.

"You have a plan?" I ask as we get in the car, Ashmodai sitting shotgun.

"The beginnings of one. Look, I'll help you find Mark P. What's-his-tits—"

"Marcus K. Dixon."

"Yeah whatever. I'll help you find him, you can deal with the consequences of whatever that turns into, and in return, you'll unbind me and leave me to my life of failed debauchery."

I give him the largest grin I can contort my mouth into.

"Amazing! I knew you'd see my side of things," I say, reaching over to squeeze his arm. He shakes me off.

"You haven't given me much of a choice. Now that only leaves us with one problem. Actually, it leaves us with many, but the first one is getting to The Fates."

"When you say Fates, is this like the Greek ones?" I ask, my mind flashing back to mythology lessons in English and History class. Also, Disney's *Hercules*. Mainly *Hercules*. I wonder if the ones he's talking about also have a single eyeball they share.

"I doubt they've ever spent time in any country on Earth. So, no. Not Greek. One of your authors, though, did come up with a pretty accurate description. It's probably because of all the drugs he did."

"Which author?"

"Something with an *A*, I think? I don't mess around with names, there's too damn many of you, but I do remember how he described them. '*One-eyed shrew of the heterosexual dollar. One-eyed shrew that winks out of the womb. One-eyed shrew that does nothing but sit on her ass and snip the intellectual golden threads of the craftsman's loom.*' Words like that stick with you."

That sounds . . . not very Disney.

"How do we get to them? I can drive." I gesture around the car we're sitting in like I'm Vanna White. "Maybe I'll look it up on . . ." my stomach drops to my feet. "I left my phone behind! I must have left it on the beach. Fuck, my parents are going to kill me!"

"You're seriously worried about that now? You're in Hell and you're worried about your parents?"

"Yes. This is the second time I've lost a phone this year."

I bang my head into the steering wheel as self-punishment. The horn goes off. Yay.

"Such a shame," he says, sounding much more sympathetic than I would expect. Suspiciously so. "We should head back to Earth and get that for you."

"Yeah, right. The second we leave Hell I know you'll find a way to make sure I never come back."

"Most people would be thrilled at the thought."

"Not me. I'm not going to abandon Marcus that easily."

Ash sighs. "It was worth a shot. Alright. At least let me distract you from the obviously traumatic experience of misplacing your phone by saying we don't need it to look up how to get to The Fates. I may be a pretty subpar demon, but I'm not *that* stupid. I'll direct you. I can't promise that the journey there will be simple, but I do know the way."

"Great." I perk back up immediately and smile at him.

"Onwards and upwards," I say, turning on the car and backing out of the parking spot.

"Backwards and downwards," he shoots back, rolling his eyes. He points to the left when I reach the parking lot's exit, and then we're off.

CHAPTER TWO

In which audiobooks and
parking lots are loathed.

Dear Marcus,

I know it's my dream to be an entertainment lawyer, but I'm not ready to stop breaking rules. Not any important rules, nothing that would end with people getting hurt, only little things. Mom says I'm a teenager who doesn't understand consequences and it will pass, and my best friend Laura says I'm an idiot trying to self-sabotage my adulthood. Typically I listen to her, Laura has always been the smart one and I think that's so fantastic, but she's wrong about this. I'm just impulsive and forget what's allowed most of the time.

With so much love,
Julia R. Tolliver

The highway is not poorly paved. It's actually quite smooth, with fresh yellow and white lines cutting through rich, black tar. The land around the road, though, is expansive, barren, and the flattest I have ever seen. Brown, dusty, and seemingly never ending, like how Elle describes Oklahoma in her podcast, except there is the addition of what appears to be tumbleweeds made of barbed wire rolling through the dirt here. Time passes, unless it doesn't. I'm starting to have a strong suspicion that it might not exist here. I wouldn't have expected to notice its absence, but I feel it, a niggling emptiness in me where the passage of time should be.

The needle on the fuel gauge has remained unchanged since we entered Hell, which is probably for the best considering I don't want to contemplate the state of the gas stations down here. Maybe it's magic, or something much worse, but I'm not about to question the seemingly endless full tank of gas. Gift horses and all that.

Ashmodai stares out the window.

"So," I begin, cutting through the thick silence that has settled in the car. He turns to me but I keep my eyes on the road. "Shax referred to you as Ash back there. Is that your nickname?"

"No."

"Oh." Silence. "Can I call you that?"

"If you insist."

I smile.

"You two must know each other pretty well if she goes around giving you nicknames and whatnot. You seem close."

"Yeah, not quite. I'm more of a plague on her restaurant and her very existence, if you want to know the truth."

"Well, you *are* a demon."

"Not a very good one."

"What does that even mean?"

Ashmodai goes quiet and returns to staring out the window, perhaps to look at the tornadoes of blood that have appeared in the distance, but then he suddenly snaps back.

"Why is your car such a stupid color?" he asks.

"Lime green? I think it's a nice color."

"Whether it's nice or not is irrelevant. It's been spray painted. Now I may not be an expert on human nature, but who in their right mind spray paints a car?"

"It's meant to be funny. Like a pun."

"A pun?"

"Yeah. Sort of. The car's name is Absinthe. I was really into *Moulin Rouge* when I got her and they drink absinthe in it, so I named the car that and decided to paint her absinthe green. That way, every drive I take will be a drug trip."

I haven't known Ash long, and he's spent most of the time so far looking disappointed, but somehow he manages to look even more so after my explanation. Which also happens to be exactly the same explanation Elle gives for her green Cadillac in the podcast, except her car has decidedly less spray paint. It's no secret that ninety percent of my personality is hewn from the media I consume, but I'd prefer Ash to think I have at least some capacity for original thought.

"That is truly awful," he says.

Quiet again. I can't take much more of this. Not to say I'm allergic to silence, but if there are many more gaps in the conversation I might have a sneezing fit to fill the dead air.

"Let's play Real or Fake," I say.

"What's that?"

"I bring up a thorny theological topic and you tell me if it's real or fake."

"That's not a real game."

"Uh, uh," I tut, trying not to look at a tree with human hands instead of leaves out the window. "We're not playing yet."

"Ha. Ha."

"Real or fake: you're a bad demon because you're new to the job."

"No," he says sternly. "We're not playing."

"Come on, it's not like we have anything better to do."

"Are you truly in the mood for games right now?"

"I don't think a second goes by when I'm not in the mood for games." This is a blatant untruth but damn does it sound cool. "Besides, the more I understand, the less I'll probably end up asking you for help. And I'll answer some questions

25

for you in return."

"There is nothing I want to know about your life. I already know more than I'd like to."

"Boo."

Ash exhales sharply. "I don't have the energy for this. Fine. What was your question?"

"Is it real or fake that you're so bad at your job because you're a newbie?"

"Going in for the kill straight out of the gate. Fine, that's real. I intend to get better at it. Hell comes with a little welcome package, some instructions on how to 'play the game,' but I've decided to ignore all of that and spend most of my time in Shax's diner."

"Doesn't that get boring?" I ask, trying to unpack the first hundred questions that answer opened up.

"So was Heaven."

Interesting.

"Real or fake: demons used to be angels."

He takes a moment to answer. I've obviously struck a nerve, and I can't tell if it's the "used to be" or the "angels" part of that question that got to him.

"Real," he says eventually, more morose than before.

"Why did you fall?" I risk asking, but he shakes his head and looks away. I drop it. We sit in silence some more as the road gently begins to veer to the right, slicing through dead land, and I almost start to feel bad about prying into his personal life. Which is something I should probably get used to considering this is Hell and badness comes with the domain.

This is Hell.

Hell. *Oh my god.*

If Laura could see me now. Laura, my best friend, with her dizzying laugh and unwavering belief in me, even when we both know I'm being ridiculous. Being ridiculous together. Having someone worth being ridiculous with.

"Why don't we listen to something!" I blurt out. "There are some CDs in the glove compartment. Hand me the one that says *Rich Bitch On the Run: Disc One."*

Burning a podcast onto CDs might be a bit old school, but the Chevy Spark came with a working player for a reason.

He does what I ask without comment and I shove the disc into the player in the dashboard. Nothing can go wrong if I'm listening to Elle; her words and the way they're spoken have almost worn new neural pathways in my brain. I know the only reason I discovered her work is because of Marcus, but I love her nearly as much. In some of my fantasies, we're best friends. In others, she's my slightly older—but still cool—mentor. In my dreams, she whisks me away from my future and takes me on the road in America, her posh British accent keeping me company as we drive out West. Now I'm finally on a road trip and it's with a disaster of a should-be mythical creature through the least welcoming place possible.

"This was created by Marcus' daughter," I explain. "She took a great American road trip when she was nineteen with a friend of hers and then talked about it in a podcast."

"Why are you telling me this?"

So I can think about anything other than what we're doing.

"Because it's one of the most important pieces of pop culture in recent history and a glimpse into the life of an amazing young woman." A pause. "Also, I try and piece together bits of Marcus's life based on hints she drops about her upbringing. She gets a bit bitchy about him, but it's all stuff that happened while she was a crazy hormonal teenager. Maybe this'll help you understand why we're rescuing him."

He grunts in response and I take it as an affirmation. I pop in the CD and press "play".

> Welcome to the first episode of *Rich Bitch On the Run*. It's me, Elle Dixon, and I am so excited to share my adventures with you. Be forewarned, I'm new to this whole podcast thing and I haven't really listened to other

ones for reference.

I'm going to give you a bit of exposition, and it goes like this:

At nineteen, I was becoming increasingly disillusioned with not only my own country, but the world as a whole. I would look at the news and see that even though Brits spoke the same language as Americans, we weren't actually communicating. I decided the only way to make any sense of it was to see it for myself.

I invited a friend from New York City, let's call her Anita, on a Great American Road Trip and she was completely onboard right away. She brought her own personal drama to the trip, of course, and I brought mine. Mainly, my father.

You all know my father. He's the only reason any of you even care about me to begin with. But this isn't about him, it's about me. Through a series of strange events involving Anita's piece of shit boyfriend, my personal angst, and having more money than common sense, we decided to not plan at all and to simply get in a car and drive. Neither of us felt like we belonged in America and we both wanted to discover it for ourselves, so we prepared to haul ass until we were far enough away from our lives that no men would be able to find us.

Yeah, right.

Anyway, I landed at JFK, bought

a 1959 candy green Cadillac with a ridiculous amount of unearned money, and drove off to find Anita. And here is where our story begins. On a road, somewhere on the East Coast between the Big Apple and middle-of-nowhere Virginia. Pavement under our wheels, my foot on the pedal, and wanderlust in our veins. We listened to Father John Misty and Aerosmith while plowing through our snacks.

One of my goals was to track down as many things that start with the words *The World's Largest* as possible. That trashy, broken, grotesque aesthetic is something I consider holy, and what I'm assuming is the only thing holding the United States together: Americana.

Yum.

The first wonder we got to was the World's Largest Apple in Winchester, Virginia. It was wooden and red, but other than that there are few ways to describe the world's largest apple other than saying it's the world's largest apple.

That night, we stayed with some family friends in a mansion in Virginia, a couple who once worked with my father. The lady warned us not to be alarmed if we heard ghosts that night because apparently that's what cows sound like when they moo, and for some godforsaken reason this house was surrounded by cows. So I stayed up late into the night, listening for ghosts.

I turn off the CD as we pass by the last dregs of the desert and enter a land of brilliant sunny skies—all blue and bright—above plush green grass the color of toxic waste.

"Are ghosts real?" I ask Ash.

He's been mostly quiet, only speaking over the podcast to reassure me that we're driving the right way. I figure that ghosts are a better talking point than asking him his opinion, knowing the answer probably won't make me happy. Years of inflicting my interests on my parents has proven that sometimes it's better not to know what others think about something you love.

"Of course ghosts are real. I've never met one personally, they're a bit rare and only hang around Earth, but I've encountered a few after they finally moved on."

"Neat."

"None of them sounded like cows."

"What did they sound like?" I ask. Ash actually seems to think about his answer for a moment.

"One of them complimented my shoes."

"Ah."

I note tall, industrial-looking buildings in the distance as the land goes from being flat and arid to hilly, and instead of only the occasional car driving by, there are more and more merging on from entrance points that appear out of nowhere, or driving towards us and veering around at the last second. The cars look normal enough, but with windows tinted so darkly I can't see who—if it is a "who"—is driving. Soon, there are dozens of lanes, and I stop being able to see what's on the side of the road over the steadily moving vehicles surrounding us.

"It looks like we've found society," I point out.

"Not so sure about that. Sentient beings? Probably. Society on the other hand? That's a lot to ask for."

I'm distracted, looking at the ridiculous number of cars in all shapes and sizes, when Ash yells, "Watch out!"

I slam my foot on the brake immediately then jerk forward to see I've barely stopped short of a line of unmoving minivans.

"You are truly an awful driver," Ash says.

"But not because I'm a woman!"

"What?" He sounds exasperated. I don't really blame him.

"I'm an awful driver because I'm an awful driver, not because I'm a woman. There's a stereotype that women drive poorly—"

"What. The. Actual. Fuck."

"And another thing—"

"Oh, shut up, would you? Pull forward. The car ahead of us is moving forward." I let this one go, and we begin creeping along.

"Are we there yet?" I ask, not wanting to contemplate what creatures could possibly be inside all the vehicles ahead of us.

"Yes, I believe we have made it to the entrance of Drizzlyland. It seems like the rumors about it are truer than I expected."

"The rumors?" I ask, and the corners of his mouth turn up the slightest amount. "You know, I think it'll be more fun if you see for yourself."

Not trusting his definition of fun, but also not having much of a choice, I continue creeping along, agonizingly slow. I always thought that traffic headed to the Boardwalk in the summer was bad, but this is beyond anything I've ever seen before.

"You're right," I say. "This traffic jam proves it. We're definitely in Hell."

"And this is only the beginning."

An infinite number of moments pass in no time at all, and I pull up next to a booth. A Wonder Bread-looking boy with perfectly coiffed brown hair leans out the window. His grin is blinding and if I were the type to make assumptions about people, I would say he looks Mormon.

"Welcome to Drizzlyland! The most enchanting place in the afterlife. How many are in your car?" His voice is bubblegum and I can practically see all of his words in a cartoon speech bubble over his head.

"Uh . . . only the two of us?" I say, as if it's a question even though I obviously know the answer.

"Isn't that swell!" He holds out a bright pink piece of paper that I have to lean almost my entire body out the window to reach. "Have the most wonderful time!" he says in that peppy voice, and then he's waving us off.

I hand the ticket to Ash and head into the parking lot we were apparently waiting in line to enter, then begin looking for an empty spot. Not the easiest task.

"What's that paper say?" I ask.

"'Drizzlyland. The Most Enchanting Place in the Afterlife.'" It's as if I can hear the capitalization. "'Rule number one: always smile. Those not smiling will be penalized. Rule number two: always speak when you are spoken to. Those ignoring others will be penalized. Rule number three: don't drink the water.'"

"That's not ominous at all." I drive farther and farther back. "Am I correct in assuming that we're about to enter a theme park?"

"Indeed we are."

I drive down one row, thinking there's an empty space, only to find that there's a really short car parked there. We continue onwards.

"I mean, it sounds like a crappy park based on those rules, but I'd say that even a crappy park is pretty damn good for Hell."

"Hell can be anything depending on the person. Sunburns, crowds, forced interaction, motion sickness, falsified happiness? The fact that you all pay money for this on Earth is proof that human beings are hardwired for masochism. Most of the people here were loners back on Earth, now forced into an eternity of the most uncomfortable social interaction with strangers imaginable. But even if these things didn't freak you out, the rules probably have a lot to do with why no one inside is going to be having a great time."

"What were they again?"

"You've got to smile, speak, and dehydrate."

"Sounds like a typical Friday night."

"Is that meant to be some sort of mature-sounding joke? Because you're literally a child."

I don't have a comeback and continue driving in silence; Ash drums his fingers along the center console as he stares out

32

the window.

"Do you want to listen to some more *Rich Bitch*?" I ask. It's obvious we're not going to find a spot any time soon.

"There's more? Haven't I been punished enough?"

"That was only the first day of adventures. She travelled for more than twenty. I'm going to skip some. All you'll miss is her passing through Knoxville, Tennessee and ending up in a hostel in Nashville for the night. Also New Orleans."

"A hostel? Isn't she stupidly rich?"

It's nice to hear that he was actually somewhat paying attention.

"Yeah, but if you live like a rich person you don't get the true American experience, and if you don't get the true American experience you can't create a wildly popular and authentic auditory masterpiece."

Ash snorts disbelievingly. "Okay. Sure."

I press "play".

CHAPTER THREE

In which rules are learnt
and immediately broken.

Welcome back, friends and enemies.
Let's pick up right as Anita and I were
driving away from New Orleans. The
rain was pouring down in sheets that
day, and eventually we couldn't even see
out of the windshield. I pulled over next
to a field of weeds and wildflowers and
got this insane urge to run around in
it. Bless Anita, she didn't say anything
along the lines of "you'll get drenched"
or "poison ivy!" but instead just asked if
I had an umbrella.

The second I opened the door, rain
poured into the car, and I jumped knee-
deep into grass, opening the umbrella
overhead. I waded around until I found
purple flowers that were beautiful
enough to be worth giving to Anita. I
yanked them from the ground and ran

back to the car, trying to keep my knees high and looking like an idiot.

These are the memories that make me the happiest. They are also the most devastating. I'd rather move on to the next tale, which you may recognize because it caused quite a stir on social media, and is also the reason why everyone found out about the trip. That's right, the Tiger Truck Stop. Anita and I needed to get gas, so we pulled off the highway into this place that seemed unassuming enough from the road. You know, it had a restaurant, a shop, an area for trucks to refuel in the back and cars in the front. Definitely the largest gas station I've ever been to. At the entrance there was a metal cage with a live tiger inside. Hanging on that cage was a sign that read "Animal rights extremists are trying to force the exhibit to be removed from the state. Please do not let this happen." There was a website to go to and sign a petition.

I was furious! Later, while Anita was driving, I posted a photo of the cage with a caption implying that maybe cages off the side of the interstate aren't the most humane places to keep tigers. The first comment that wasn't someone asking what the hell I was doing in Louisiana was an old man saying how the animal would tear me to shreds if it could and that I should be more worried about taxes.

Some thoughts on this:

One, I am perfectly capable of being worried about both animal rights and taxes, I'm just lucky enough to not have to be worried about the latter. Also, I don't even pay American taxes and those were definitely the ones being referred to.

Two, I appreciate you all coming to my defense in the way that you did, but you didn't have to drive that man off of social media.

Or call PETA on the owners.

Or chain yourselves to the cage.

Or start an international campaign to save one tiger in Louisiana.

Who knows, maybe the owners appreciated all the publicity those months of protests and complaints brought—I doubt they had ever been interviewed by that many news stations before—but considering it ended with their tiger in a zoo, I'm assuming I'm high up on their shit list.

All I know is that cages are my biggest fear, and if I was that tiger, I would rather be dead than inside one. Robert Louis Stevenson said something along the lines of "when a devil has been caged, he comes out roaring." I'm misquoting, but the point is that locking the living away damages everyone.

Ash grunts something that's nearly a laugh in response to that line, and I click off the podcast. "Are you laughing at her not knowing her *Jekyll and Hyde* quotes or the fact that she's talking about devils?"

"Devils, obviously. I enjoy the ridiculousness of her implying they can be caged."

"You can't capture a devil?" I ask.

"No way. Keeping so-called 'devils' locked up is what created them to begin with."

"Then what have I done to you? Isn't this binding a sort of cage?" I ask as we continue this Kafkaesque jaunt through the parking lot, knowing that I'm playing with fire. Ash is silent for a moment, then chooses to ignore what I said and continue explaining only what he wants to explain. I am starting to suspect he enjoys hearing himself talk.

"Take Lucifer. The big guy. They say he worked harder than anyone up in Heaven and when the time came for someone to get a promotion, the equivalent of the CEO promoting his recently hired son happened. God decides that people are his new favorites and gives them the Earth. Shax thinks that's when Lucifer started to see the bars of the cage. He got out. Now the devils are free and it's the angels who are prisoners. Most of them don't know it. I didn't."

That's a lot to take in. Charming to know that Ash at least likes his boss. Is boss the right term? He seems to understand business structures, considering the CEO analogy.

"Are you and Lucifer friends?"

"Absolutely not. We've never even met. Last I heard, he's hanging out on Earth. There was some hearsay that he's doing a stint as a violinist somewhere."

"Huh."

I take some time to consider this and how Ash so obviously wants to talk. Does he have any friends? That poor boy must have so much pent up inside him. I never thought about how lonely it must be to be a demon, especially a bad one. Maybe my secondary objective, after freeing Marcus, will be to encourage Ash to continue opening up to me. It'll be good career practice.

Plus, I don't like it when people are lonely.

There's a lot going on in my head, from thoughts of the Bible's accuracy to ruminations on the ridiculousness of this parking lot. Fragments of ideas pinging back and forth like silver balls in a pinball machine, erratic and uncontrollable, but exciting. Beautiful. The cars go on forever, and everything about this place is uncomfortable and frightening. But, then again, so is high school. So was the hospital.

An empty spot comes into view and I pull in, saying a little "thank you" to no one in particular. Stepping out of the car feels like walking into a sauna; the heat is thick and disgusting. I try not to grimace, pretend like I've stepped off an airplane in Orlando, and begin the long trek out of the parking lot. Signs, mounted upside-down, point us towards the entrance. There's a random smattering of other people navigating the area who keep their distance from us as we all follow the signs.

"The Fates will be inside the park?" I ask.

Ash nods. "Should be. It's only a matter of tracking them down. But considering this is Hell for people who wanted to be left alone back on Earth, there shouldn't be a shortage of people to ask."

"This reminds me of when Laura and I went to Florida last summer. There was a convention for Fletcher Fatale fans and we spent a few nights in the theme parks, too."

"If you're trying to convince me you aren't as idiotic as I previously thought, this story definitely isn't helping."

We walk in silence, me enjoying the bright sunshine coming from no discernible source, Ash trying his best to look cool, with hands in his pockets and everything.

Until he decides to pry into my personal life and asks, "Laura?"

"My best friend. Only friend, actually. We wear obsession beautifully."

Laura and I bonded as hormonal, acne-covered high schoolers who felt they had no one else to turn to. Together we discovered Fletcher Fatale, and eventually all the works of Marcus K. Dixon. All we did was hype one another up and feed into the obsession until one day, Laura had written a novel-length, smutty, Alternate Universe fanfiction about Fletcher Fatale and Ferdinand Ferdinand that became so popular, she got some fans herself. Laura was recognized in a bookstore once, and it made me feel like I was friends with a celebrity.

It was one of the most wonderful, exhilarating things I've ever felt.

Now she seems to be slowly weaning off of Marcus K. Dixon-related hobbies and I hope whatever our friendship looked like before we found him can survive. Honestly, I'm not even sure what we used to talk about all the time.

We'll figure it out, though. We have to. We're best friends.

The blue sky of this world turns increasingly yellow and sickly the closer we get to the entrance of Drizzyland, and I try to clear my mind of any Laura-related thoughts. I haven't even been gone that long and I'm starting to miss her.

The parking lot ends and is replaced by grey cement and a theme park entrance with flags, awnings, and poorly dressed employees. There's a long line of people waiting to get in, walking single file through a metal detector. As we approach them, Ash nudges me.

"Now is probably a good time to start smiling."

Glancing at the people in front of and behind us, diverse as the cover of an Earth science textbook, I realize they all have insane grins plastered on their faces that don't reach their eyes. Ash is smiling, too. I don't like how it looks on him, and I'm certain the smile I force my mouth into is equally disturbing.

"Do we have a game plan?" I ask as we inch forward.

"Get in. Follow the rules. Talk to everyone we see because they're forced to talk back. Shouldn't take too long to find The Fates and interrogate them about the location of your man."

"Love it."

Another Mormon-looking boy waves me through a metal detector that doesn't seem to actually do anything, and then Ash and I are corralled inside.

There's a castle in the distance, lemon yellow with blue

spires, and a cobblestone road leading up to it, branching off to unknown locations concealed by towering animal-shaped topiaries.

"Something's wrong with this place," I say, feeling hot and thirsty, but also like the world is throbbing. There's music being piped out of an unidentifiable location. I recognize it from an old Hollywood movie musical whose name I can't remember.

"Something's always wrong. It's Hell."

We walk slowly down the street, me continuously taking up more of Ash's personal space than he's probably comfortable with. It's bizarre to see a place so methodically upbeat and merry. There are people selling balloons, hundreds of them tied around one hand and undoubtedly cutting off circulation, and middle-aged men in brightly colored T-shirts. Everyone has the biggest smile and the dullest eyes. Once we are at the end of the street, standing at the base of the castle, Ash decides it's time to take action. Off to the side, a janitor in a brilliantly white jumpsuit and black sneakers empties a trash can. Ash jerks his head towards the man, questioningly, and I nod.

"Hey there," Ash calls out as we walk over. "Can we ask you something?"

The janitor straightens his back and squints at us, which looks even more demented with his smile.

"Why, of course you can!"

Ash leans against the trash can, admittedly looking quite cool, and says, "Ashmodai here. Demon. High ranking. Really high ranking. Like, so high ranking most other demons have never even heard of me. My friend and I are looking for The Fates and, while I could, of course, locate them myself with my omniscient demon abilities that definitely do whatever I want them to, it suits me better to hear their location from you."

The janitor actually seems to buy into that load of nonsense.

"I'm sorry, sir, but I can't tell you that."

"Assume I outrank whoever is making you keep it a secret and tell me the location of The Fates. I know you know where they are."

The man is silent for a bit too long, his eyes large and round. Ash straightens and grabs him by the shoulders.

"Tell me!"

The janitor's smile falters, just for a single moment as Ash shakes him, but that's all it takes. Before I can even process what is going on, it's not Ash's hands on his shoulders anymore, but instead those of a rat monster and a blonde woman wearing a tiara, forcibly dragging the man away.

"No! No! No!" he screams, starting to kick his legs as they are swept out from under him. He struggles, but it makes no difference, and the three of them disappear around a hedge, and the screams grow increasingly distant.

"And that's why you can't stop smiling," Ash says after a moment. Looking around, I see that everyone else who watched this scene play out never let their grins fall. The fact that mine is still intact is truly shocking.

"What are they going to do to him?" I ask, and Ash shrugs.

"Did that sound like the screams of someone who's going off to be gently reprimanded?" He straightens out his margarita shirt. "Best not to think about these things."

I nod and slowly walk towards a metal bridge over an obviously man-made lake. "That wasn't very helpful. Maybe we should split up and see how we do."

"Are you kidding me?" Ash says. "Have you forgotten you bound me to your side on the threat of extreme pain? There're enough other people getting tortured here, you don't need to add me to the mix."

He points to a man who has blobs of millennial-pink cotton candy stuck randomly all over himself, looking on the verge of being violently ill but still with a near-sadistic grin on his grey face.

"You're right."

And so, we walk in the blazing heat that grows increasingly intense, exacerbated by the glistening metal.

Step after step after step. Trembling body and trembling thoughts.

41

My face hurts. Now I understand why Marcus never smiles for photo shoots. We enter some area that appears to be outer space themed, or maybe it's meant to be futuristic. It's hard to think about that with how disgustingly hot it is and how much my cheeks ache. It's like when new shoes cut into the backs of your feet or you really need to use the bathroom, and it becomes the only thing you can focus on. There's no way I can keep this up. But I remember the princess' dead eyes. A stuffed rat tail. There are worse things than aching cheeks.

Like doctor's needles and dead loves. Or punishments from an unknown god.

A ride to my left spins impossibly fast, like a Musical Express with rocket ship-shaped cars. The line to get on is enormous, spilling out of the roped-off queue and zigzagging haphazardly into the walkway. The people riding are blurs of color.

When I was in the hospital, they made me rate my pain on a scale of one to ten. Pain is easy to categorize like that. Every morning, a nurse would ask for a number, and that number matched an obvious color, and it was easy. What I'm experiencing now is much worse, though: discomfort. Discomfort is stretchy and formless, spilling out into the rest of my body until it feels like it's glowing bright orange. There's so much to look at but none of it will stick in my brain, which is about to melt straight out of my ears. My cheeks are ready to seize up with exertion.

Ash walks up to someone waiting in the line and I linger not too far away.

In the distance, past a bright green hot dog cart and a man dressed as an alien, I spot a glistening water fountain.

If I get to that fountain, everything will be okay. A cool stream of water and this perversion of reality will be bearable. I know it.

The world moves in slow motion.

One foot in front of the other foot. Step by step, the air reverberating around my ears, I cross to the fountain. The part of me screaming that this is against the rules is indecipherable from the part that has been screaming nonstop since Ash appeared on the beach.

There is something to remember about Ash.

I'll try to think of it after I've had a drink of water.

As I get closer, music from the arcade behind the water fountain grows louder, a repetitive synth song. Discotheque? Techno? It's futuristic and pointed.

Stand in front of the fountain. Press the button. A stream of clear water bursts out so beautifully I want to cry. Bend over. It is delicious.

It is wonderful.

It . . . it burns.

I throw myself away from the fountain, but it's too late. Burning. Burning down my throat and in my eyes. The world is vibrating. Trembling.

Cracking.

I look at my hands and my fingernails are crawling. They grow legs and crawl over my hands, like grotesque insects and my worst nightmare. A scream. It continues. Is that my voice?

No. It sounds too horrible. It sounds like the end of the world.

The colors flash around me and I run even though my legs don't take me anywhere. The air writhes like the wriggling ground beneath my feet.

Cowboys.

There's a cowboy grabbing my arm.

Shake. Shake. I try to shake him off.

Why won't this girl stop screaming? There's a man screaming, too. There's a whole lot of noise and I'd think about it more except black balls have started rolling across my line of sight. Bouncing all around me.

I wish I would throw up. Maybe it would make me feel better. Except I can't throw up because he's here. Fletcher Fatale. Marcus. His Hollywood white teeth and deep brown eyes are right there. My eyes roam down his arm, which is in such a beautiful sleeve, attached to a blue fitted suit covering my favorite body. I open my mouth to call to him but yarn starts spilling out in long, red lengths. An endless amount of rough, scratching yarn drags itself out of my throat and it's not Fletcher Fatale. It's Laura. But Laura with my mother's face and my father's hands. I know it's her, though, and I can't bear for her to see me like this. "Stop hiding, Jules," she says. "Stop hiding from yourself."

Something is coming. It vibrates through the air and into my bones. A parade. The electroshock colors get brighter and brighter, a drum bangs steadily, and then—nothing.

CHAPTER FOUR

In which memories are mind-numbing
and hospitals do not heal.

Dear Marcus,

    Sometimes, when I have to stop living in my fantasies and acknowledge that I may not be able to marry you one day, I think about marrying another one of your fans. Laura and I recently got back from a convention where I looked at every boy dressed as a different version of you, and a few dressed as Ferdinand Ferdinand, and tried to feel something. Nothing happened. I only have eyes for you. Laura, on the other hand—she'll step out with any boy that has a cape strapped around his neck. I'd say I wish I was more like her, but I have different priorities, I guess.

Looking ahead,
Julia R. Tolliver

"Jules. Jules. You have to wake up. Please, Jules. I can't."
    Eyes open. The same yellow skies fill my vision. Those

yellow skies and Ash, grinning like he's happy to see me, but then I remember that he has to smile like that or else something terrible will happen to him. Blinking, I quickly stretch my lips into some bastardization of a smile and attempt to sit up, the cement walkway rough against my mostly bare legs.

"What—"

"You drank the water," Ash cuts me off. "You ran off and drank the water and abandoned me."

"Sorry," I tell him, looking around. I'm back in the outer space section. My fingernails also appear to be back where they belong, although I do still feel like I have to vomit.

"No, I don't think you understand, Jules. You *left* me. Have you forgotten that you bonded me to your side? If you run off I feel like I've been thrown into a lake of acid. I'd like to see you try and maintain a smile through agony like that."

"Oh god," I say, running a hand through my hair. "I'm sorry. Did they punish you?"

"Yeah. They did." Ash straightens himself up next to me.

"What did they do to you?"

He sighs. "They dragged me away and did. . . awful things. Something useful actually did come out of it, though. I know where The Fates are."

Is it really going to be that easy? It can't be. He looks broken and I begin to worry about these "awful things" they did to him. The guy's annoying but not *that* annoying.

"What did they do to you?" I ask again, trying to sound more sympathetic for him than excited that he got us one step closer to my end goal.

"Apparently when you break the smiling rule, the punishment is that they force you to relive your worst memories. Who better to access your past than The Fates? They did a job on me and dumped me back here before I could think through the pain. But while I was there, I caught a glimpse of one of The Fates and her golden scissors."

"That's great! We should go right now."

I stand, Ash staring at me and not offering a hand to help or

46

anything. He's uneasy, it's not difficult to tell, and we don't talk about it as we walk past people trying obviously not to look at us. I let him lead the way to another area of the park, a Wild West section. Whoever designed this place must be marginally clever; the science fiction paraphernalia blends almost seamlessly into saloon doors and cowboy hats. A masterpiece of engineering and distraction. Music comes from rocks and trees as the cement ground turns to dirt—a clean sort, if that's possible—beneath our feet. There are thirteen lanterns and a lasso hanging from a tree and for a moment, I think it's a noose. Maybe I should rethink what I said about the designers' cleverness. Who hangs a lasso from a tree as a design choice?

"How did you find me again?" I ask.

"If you haven't noticed, no one else here is lying on the ground. You weren't too hard to miss."

"How long was I out for?"

"No idea." Ash sighs. "I suspect the only reason you were able to be 'out' to begin with is because you've got that living body of yours. I'm still trying to figure out why you weren't immediately busted for not smiling. Maybe Hell was so thrown by having an unconscious girl they decided to completely ignore it."

I nod, taking it all in. Passing out is not a particularly uncommon occurrence in my life, so it's no surprise that the drugged, acidic water, or whatever the hell it was, would trigger one of my legendary fainting spells. Sometimes, I think about my body like it's a puppy doing something rotten, or a child acting up. *Stop it, now!* I chastise my limbs, and my blood, and my brain. *Do as you're told.*

It rarely listens.

A group of aging white men and two women dressed as cowgirls begin line dancing to our left, and for the first time, I begin to fully accept that I am in Hell. As we continue walking, swinging saloon doors and shotguns slowly begin morphing into swords and ships. A pirate-themed area. Fun. There's water lapping in the distance and seagulls that appear primed and ready to shit on anyone that walks beneath them. Judging by their glassy eyes, they're probably animatrons, which will make the shitting even more impressive.

"What did they show you?" I ask Ash. "The Fates?"

"Nothing much. My memories don't work the same way as the humans they punish." He's lying.

"What did they show you?" I try again.

"It had to do with my demotion." Ash's bastard exterior falls away. Just a little. Just enough for me to accept that it really is a facade.

"Your demotion?"

"My fall. What else were you expecting?"

I've decided to stop expecting anything anymore.

Ash takes me by the arm and leads me away from the main walkway. Ducking behind a faded statue of Blackbeard and a packed gift shop, we make our way to a secret back entrance of a square, industrial-looking building. The door is obviously an emergency exit, although I don't know what emergencies they could possibly be anticipating.

Ash tries the handle to no avail, then begins pushing against the door with both hands before ramming into it with his shoulder. The only other place I've seen people try that is the movies.

"Can I give it a go?" I ask, and he gestures for me to go ahead. Similar results. "Do you have a credit card?"

He gives me another look of abject disappointment.

"No, I don't have a credit card."

"Damn it."

I frequently break into the supply closet where late passes are stored at school, but the method I use requires a credit card or student ID. These doors are undoubtedly more complex than the ones purchased by the American education system, but it would have been worth a try. Not that the now-implied lack of capitalism in the afterlife isn't exciting.

I will my brain to think of something useful and begin running through other potential ideas, finally landing on one that might not be totally awful.

"Crazy idea," I start. "What if we stop smiling and let ourselves get dragged inside? If we both go together, you won't be in massive amounts of pain this time, and it'll be easy to break away and talk to The Fates."

He pauses for a moment, considering, then nods.

"That's a truly awful idea, especially considering we aren't even sure if the rules apply to you, oxygen-breather. Let's do it. Hold on to me." He opens up his arms as if waiting for a big hug.

"What?"

"If they can't separate us, they might drag us away together. Hug me. I'm sorry, but I'm not risking bond-separation agony and having to sit through Ashmodai's Greatest Failures again."

Fair enough. I stretch out my arms and beckon him to me with my chin, my smile becoming slightly more genuine for a moment, and he steps forward to embrace me. I don't want to say anything sappy like *This is the first time someone has hugged me in months* but that doesn't make it any less of a fact. It can be strange to have someone's arms around you, to not be able to control the limbs you're wrapped in. Squished tightly together, I look up at him and he looks down at me.

"Stop smiling in three. Two. One."

We both drop our grins. It feels like paradise. For the first time since we've gotten here, there's a smile in Ash's eyes, if nowhere else.

Two pirates are on us in seconds. I grip Ash even tighter, hooking my fingers into his shirt, and for a moment, I'm reminded of hugging my father. A girl pirate grabs me from behind, wrapping her ruffled arms around my waist, and it's obvious they're trying to separate us. Ash must be experiencing the same thing because he digs into my back so hard, I'm certain he's leaving marks. I jump up and wrap my legs around him in the best imitation of a koala I can manage.

Our assailants are unexpectedly strong, though, and I am yanked viciously off of Ash. I kick my feet in an attempt to regain my footing as I see white arms wrap around him, standing in contrast to his skin and reminding me of bleach, or a disease. Something with the power to kill. It makes no difference and I still end up half dragged to the front of the building by a redheaded woman in a surprisingly cute, striped dress. The double doors open automatically and, once my eyes adjust to the dark, I realize we are inside a theater. A small, crappy one—exactly what you would expect to see in a theme park. There are only about twenty rows of seats with people slouched randomly throughout, although there are more sitting in aisle seats than anywhere else.

I get pushed into one of those, and before I can even think to fight back or look around for Ash, my wrists are strapped down to the armrests. Everything is coarse and scratches against my bare skin.

Oh no. Oh god no. Hopefully Ash is faring better than I am. Hopefully he's found a way to—

> *Jules has to go to the bathroom. Usually she would wait until the end of class, but not today. She digs the hall pass out of her bag and stands up to cross over to her science teacher. The words "I need" have not even left her lips before she passes out, hitting her head on a lab table on the way down.*
>
> *The next thing Jules knows, she is sitting on a stool, slumped over the teacher's desk, and every other twelve-year-old is staring at her. There's a voice in the hallway, her teacher's voice, saying something about someone being "pale as a ghost."*
>
> *What an ugly cliché.*
>
> *A wheelchair is brought into the room by a nurse and Jules is moved into it. Only moments after she is wheeled into the hallway, the bell rings and suddenly they are navigating through a sea of a million preteens. People ask what happened and Jules ignores them as the nurse shoos them away to*

the best of her ability.

In the nurse's office are yellow lights and blue Gatorade.

Someone brings her the bag she left abandoned in the classroom, but the hall pass was lost along the way. For the rest of the month, Jules is not permitted to leave her classes to go to the bathroom without it.

I take a deep breath, gasping as I am dragged out of the memory, my head throbbing with what I just witnessed. The sheer, world-ending ache of being an embarrassed twelve-year-old kid. I fling my head around wildly, looking for Ash but only seeing the limp bodies of strangers slouched in seats, twitching in pain where they are tied down, but then—

There isn't a DVD player in her room at the hospital. Laura burned Jules a DVD of the most recent episode of Bluecoat—*featuring a cameo by Marcus K. Dixon*—*but there isn't a way to watch it. Jules prays instead, holding the DVD to her heart with the hand that doesn't have an IV inserted in it.*

Marcus, I'm sorry I can't watch this right now. I promise I'm still your biggest fan.

She wishes she could say it's only the morphine causing her to hold make-believe conversations with an actor in her head, but she's been doing this for months now. Some people never get too old for imaginary friends, even if said imaginary friend is a real person that they've never actually met.

Jules cannot bear to be alone.

It's three in the morning and the girl on the opposite side of the room divider is shouting for a bedpan.

Jules wants morphine and they won't give it to her. She can't remember why. She presses the call button just for fun. She thinks about bathtubs and toasters and British men and doesn't sleep.

These are more than memories. My vision is going blurry with the exertion of reliving them, and I don't even bother trying to scream for Ash as my head bobs drunkenly on my neck, too weak to hold it up.

There's a bonfire in a backyard in New Jersey. Jules can feel its heat on her face and—

"Ow! What the fuck?" Ash slapped me. *Ash slapped me!*

"Ash!" I breathe out as he pulls a pair of gleaming gold scissors from his back pocket and uses them to slice through my bindings. I try to shake the fog out of my brain, and hope he didn't get taken far from me. He doesn't look too much the worse for wear.

"You can thank me later," he says, yanking me out of the seat. "I just had a run-in with a particularly unhappy Fate, and not the one we need. I think any sort of diplomatic approach to this is out. We have got to get backstage."

He takes my hand and we're off, down the lushly carpeted aisle and past row after row of people, some completely paralyzed and others twitching in discomfort and pain. A few are dressed as theme park employees, while others seem to be guests. They look expressionless and dead. They *are* dead. We get to the end of the aisle but there aren't any stairs to the stage.

Ash lifts me up to sit on the edge and I roll to my feet like some sort of off-brand James Bond. He gracelessly pulls himself up by his arms, like when you try to get out of a pool without using the ladder, and I grab one of his hands to help him. We don't waste any time on the stage; Ash keeps ahold of my hand and heads to the wings of the theater.

Empty. Dark. Covered in dust. The only light is musky and dim, emanating from somewhere indiscernible up above us, and the green of the glow tape beneath our feet.

There's a loud, metallic bang overhead.

"Over here," Ash says, and heads to a rusted spiral staircase that reminds me of fire escapes and penitentiaries. Every step we take clangs tinnily up to the ceiling and I wonder if we should be quieter.

"Quicker, quicker," Ash goads from in front of me. We clamber up, and once Ash reaches the top, I hear a triumphant "Ah ha!" like he's some sort of detective on a bad television program. Soon, I see the cause of his excitement: a beautiful woman, dressed all in black with long, flowing hair. Back in the day, a questionable male writer might have called her "svelte" or a "femme fatale."

"One-eyed shrew of the heterosexual dollar," Ash says, half to me, but also to get her attention.

She turns, facing away from a small black and white screen now illuminating her dimly from behind. Indeed, she does only have one eye, with a small swirling nebula residing in the hole where her right one should be. It's as if instead of there being a skull underneath her face, there's a window to another galaxy or universe.

"You stole something of my sister's," she says, except there is a delay between when she speaks and the words reaching my ears. Like we're on a video call and she's lagging. "Give it back."

"She wouldn't answer my question," Ash says. "Maybe you will. Where is Marcus K. Dahmer?"

"Dixon," I correct.

"Where is Marcus K. *Dixon*?" he repeats, glancing at me and rolling his eyes before pulling the scissors out of his back pocket and holding them up to the woman menacingly. He oozes much more Big Dick Energy than I know him to actually possess.

She laughs, a scratchy sort of end-times laugh.

"Bold of you to threaten me with the very thing I'm asking for."

53

"Yeah, well, my fists alone haven't ever managed to strike fear into the hearts of Hell's finest. These scissors are considerably pointier. Now, there's no way you guys don't know where Marcus is. I admit, I don't particularly want to meet the guy either, but that's life. Well, death. Whatever. Tell me and you can have your scissors back."

"That knowledge isn't typically made public," she says, giving him a once-over, "to low-caliber demons such as yourself. Besides, you're asking the wrong Fate. My sister keeps all of that information."

"Then I guess I'll have to go find where she's hidden it. What kind of demon would I be if I didn't break the rules?"

"A better one than this. You act like this will end well for you. Ashmodai, we are the past. We are the present. We are the future. There is nothing you are or will be that we do not cradle in our hands every moment of every day. You will give me the scissors."

"No."

Before I have time to process it, the Fate reaches out a bony arm, now stretched to an impossible length, and grabs me by the hair, yanking back. I let out a grunt and flail my arms, trying not to lose balance as I feel my hair coming out at the roots. A small, distressed moan escapes my lips.

"Shit," Ash squeaks out. I can't see him anymore; my eyes are trained on the ceiling above us as I try hopelessly to wrench myself from her grip, the pain increasing with each tug. I yank my head over and over, making everything so much worse, until suddenly, I'm free.

I feel lighter.

Ash pushes me back to the stairs as the beautiful woman screams.

"What . . ." I begin, but don't finish, too preoccupied with getting away. Something's wrong.

"Did you cut off my hair?" I screech, angrily eyeing the scissors he is holding. My hands fly up to touch my head as I race down the spiral staircase, each step clanking murderously loud in the otherwise silent theater.

"You're welcome," is his only response.

I reach the bottom of the stairs only to see that the way is blocked by the beautiful Fate. She has a fistful of my hair, knotted and grotesque.

"Ashmodai," she intones, looking straight through me. "You are about to do something incredibly stupid. Before you do, please know this: fuck you."

And then Ash pushes past me and stabs her in the neck with the scissors. Black tar squirts out and hits me directly in the face.

Gross.

She screams and falls back; Ash takes me by the arms and nearly carries me onto the stage. We stumble under the blindingly white lights.

"We have to get to the other end of the theater," he tells me, stumbling towards the edge of the stage. I follow, pained screeches reverberating dangerously loud against the wall. We jump off the edge and run up the aisle, past people who are too involved in their own pain to realize the world around them is falling apart.

Once we get to the back row, instead of doing the sane thing and getting out as quickly as possible, Ash veers to the right and jumps into a little booth centered behind the last row of seats. Without thinking, I climb in after him, throwing my body over the edge in a less-than-graceful way.

"What are you doing?" I whisper-shout as he crouches down and looks at all the computers and switchboards on a desk within. I don't know a lot about theater, but I imagine this would typically relate to lights or sounds or something.

"The information we need is in here, on something physical. It has to be."

"It does?" I ask, but before I can further express my confusion, someone grabs me from behind.

"Absolutely fucking not," I shout.

There is no way this bitch, whoever she is, is going to make me lose even more of my hair. I kick back with one foot as hard as possible and seem to throw my attacker off. Turning, I see a skeletal woman with talons for fingers, unclothed and sallow skinned. She's tall and growing taller. She also looks like her bones will snap in half if she tries to make any sudden movements. Backing up, I bump into Ash, who is still crouched and rooting around through the shelves of the booth.

"If you don't find what you need in the next three seconds, we're leaving," I say. He stands straight, holding a cardboard box. "Got it! Now move."

He jumps over the side of the booth, then reaches over to help pull me out as the skeleton lady continues growing larger and larger. She swipes at us with well-sharpened claws and takes a long but unsteady step in our direction as we make a break for the front door.

"When we get outside," Ash says, taking me by one hand and holding tight to the box with his other, "we run and we keep on running. Don't stop until we get to the car. I don't care how tired your legs get because anything these shrews could do to us is infinitely worse."

My hair is proof enough of that.

We barrel out the door in a flurry of limbs. Outside, it's almost as offensively bright as it was under those harsh stage lights, but I'm too preoccupied with the fact that we're holding hands and running like Fletcher Fatale and Ferdinand Ferdinand do in all of my favorite fan art to really process it. Not bothering with the pretense of smiling, we run, dodging out of the way of costumed characters and grinning employees who keep grabbing at us. They don't seem used to anyone fighting back. Occasionally, Ash takes something out of the box, looks at it for a moment, then throws it at someone in pursuit. Whatever the projectiles are, they don't make much of a difference.

There's an ear-splitting crash behind us. Like every good tragic hero, I make the mistake of looking back only to see the Fate, now grown impossibly large, bursting out of the roof of the theater.

"She's coming for us!" I scream, or at least, get as close to screaming as I can in my winded state.

"No shit. But she's big, which means she's unwieldy and can't follow us out of the park. Hopefully. I would imagine not."

"You're not certain?"

Ash doesn't answer and we run through the science fiction area, my legs slowly turning to jelly beneath me.

"Come on," he urges. "I'm not having any fun either."

"I'm going as fast as I can!"

Horrible, booming footsteps grow louder and louder as we hit the cobblestone street until it's obvious that the Fate is right behind us. I really wish Ash hadn't left those scissors embedded in the beautiful woman's neck, considering they had been an effective weapon.

"We're nearly there," he whispers, more to himself than me. "Here, take this."

He hands me the box and, while running and never letting go of my hand, reaches out and grabs a popcorn cart. One-handed, he drags it along before shoving it directly into one of the giant legs we're almost next to. There's a guttural cry, seemingly more out of shock than pain, but it buys us enough time to make it to the entrance, over the turnstiles, and out of Drizzlyland.

We keep going, not even taking a moment to celebrate, flying over hot pavement through the endless sea of cars. Eventually, we both seem to accept that the world has calmed down enough for us to catch our breath, and we slow to a stop in unison.

I bend over, hands on my knobby teenage knees and box on the ground while I wheeze like an old man.

"These lungs ain't what they used to be," I say in an attempt at a joke, but Ash either doesn't get it or doesn't hear.

Instead, he lunges to grab the box from where I had set it down on the pavement and holds it in one arm while reaching in with the other. He pulls objects out, looks at them, grumbles something that I can't hear, then throws them over his shoulder. After a moment, I realize that they are sleek black flash drives.

"What's on those?" I ask softly, taking him by the arm

and slowly guiding us back towards the car. He takes a look at another, says "nope," and tosses it away. If anyone wants to come after us, they'll have a well-defined path to follow.

"If I'm correct, and I probably am, one of these is a list of the damned. A map of all who inhabit Hell, including your Marcus K. Dixon. This land may be chaotic, but someone has to keep it in order." He throws another flash drive behind him. "I came across the first Fate, shrew number one, while you were strapped to that chair. She gave me the idea that this information doesn't only exist in the minds of The Fates, but is also stored in something tangible. Just our luck that we had to encounter all three of them before I started actually using my brain and put the pieces together."

He goes to throw another one of the flash drives but I snatch it from his hand before it can go flying. Written on the side, in small print with a Sharpie, is "Sleep Paralysis Demons—Chromatically." As I go to throw it, a long strand of hair—out of place, horrible, and one of the only pieces that hadn't been chopped off—gets caught in my mouth. I spit it out with what must be a disgusted expression on my face. Ash remains preoccupied with the box I've concluded must be bottomless. I can see Absinthe's bright green paint in the distance when I hear his "Ah ha!" and I pray that isn't his new catchphrase because my heart won't be able to take it.

"Found it," he exclaims, holding a flash drive above his head and promptly dropping the box on the ground. Flash drives fall out and scatter all around us.

"That one will show us where Marcus is?"

"It should." Ash lowers his arm and reads the side of the flash drive out loud. "The Damned—Alphabetically and Regionally."

"That's going to take a while to read through," I say, finally reaching the car and opening the driver's side door. I can already feel the sweltering heat that awaits us inside. "I imagine there are a lot of people down here from, you know, all of recorded history."

"Unrecorded, too," Ash adds rather unhelpfully. "But you're

jumping the gun in terms of Things to Worry About. Who cares how long it's going to take to scroll through all that nonsense? I'm trying to think of where we're going to find a computer to stick this into."

"Oh." I pause for a second. "You make a good point." I fold myself into the car, my ass burning uncomfortably on the hot leather seat. When we're both settled with seat belts buckled, I turn to him and ask, "Where to now?"

"How should I know? This is your idiotic scheme."

"Look, I know you're the self-proclaimed worst demon of all time—"

"Now I never said—"

"But I think we can both agree that you have considerably more experience in navigating Hell than I do."

"No, I don't. Alright? I've been around since before the Earth cooled. Since before Earth was an idea and cooling could even be conceptualized. I'm an angel and I have been an angel for a millennia before millennia began, except I'm not an angel anymore! I'm a goddamn demon. Lucky humans. You leave your countries, your homelands, and still get to say 'I'm American' or 'I'm Ecuadorian.' Not me. I'm just a demon now."

Well, that was definitely a lot of words. Silence. One moment. Two.

"I still don't know where to—"

"Drive. We'll figure it out on the road."

"No. We'll figure it out now. We need a computer, right? Fine. Where's the nearest computer?"

Ash closes his eyes and thinks, then says with endlessly melodramatic exasperation, "Do hospitals have computers?"

My heart stops at the word *hospital*. I try not to let discomfort show on my face.

"Usually they do."

"Saint Abaddon Hospital. I'll direct you there."

"See? That wasn't so difficult."

I reverse, a heavy silence descending over the car. Ash crosses his arms and shifts his entire body towards the passenger window, staring out of it like a petulant teen. I know this because I am a petulant teen who has frequently pulled this same crap on her mother. The silence stretches as I exit the parking lot and, judging by the parking attendant's face, people leaving is not a frequent occurrence. I find myself having to drive on the shoulder to get out. Every single lane is full of cars entering the park and none exiting. Eventually, we make it back to the main road—I guess it's a highway—and I turn in the direction Ash points. Having a hospital as the destination really puts a damper on driving.

Sometimes, I feel like I don't own my body, that I'm merely renting it. If it actually belonged to me, it would do what I want. Instead, I'm what doctors refer to as a "medical mystery." It's certainly not the worst thing someone can be; for example, I could be someone who thinks Fletcher Fatale belongs with Mary Jolene instead of Ferdinand Ferdinand. I still function like everyone else and no one can tell I'm broken. Anything that's invisible and hasn't killed me yet is as good as nonexistent. I force it to be.

What I refer to as my Big Hospitalization happened last summer. I've been a fainter my entire life, and Laura used to call me a fainting goat because of all those memes of goats getting scared and passing out. I'm like that, except no one can figure out what triggers my fainting spells. It certainly isn't fear. What landed me in the ER wasn't the fainting, but the fact that I lost consciousness at a garage sale, taking out an entire table of knickknacks as well as half of my face. There's barely any scarring left, but since that incident I've been painfully aware that it isn't the fainting I should be worried about, but what I might hit on the way down.

They kept me in the hospital to try and figure out what was wrong with me. A doctor told my mother she should have brought me in the first time I passed out for no reason, not the twentieth. She cried and said it was just something I did and no one ever thought about it. She called herself a bad mother, but I know she didn't really believe it.

At least there are some good things about hospitals. I like the long hallways they wheel you down, and the volunteers who refill the water jugs. But I don't like exams and scans and being someone's failed hypothesis.

I have a feeling that the hospital down here will be much more oriented towards needles and knives than smiling nurses with green Jell-O.

We reach a fork in the road and diverge from our previous route, getting that much closer to Saint Abaddon Hospital. The land is cracked and dead like someone's eczema. Everything is flat, apart from sticks protruding out of the dead earth with tips that wiggle like fingers. They probably are fingers.

The car remains silent, the gentle hum of an old engine filling the air.

Elle wouldn't be ignoring the situation like I am now, the way Ash is sitting quietly, looking like he swallowed something horrible. She wouldn't let him be pissy like this. She would sense that he wants to talk about whatever the hell is going on inside that brain of his because keeping secrets is just some weird form of demonic posturing. Time for a bit of lawyerly diplomacy.

"You know, I'm really scared to go to college," I say after he indicates a turn. "I'll walk into Hell any day, but John Jay campus? They're going to have to drag me there. Which is ridiculous. I sent in the application myself and it's in New York. I don't even have to get on a plane to go there. You'd expect me to be happy to leave New Jersey. I mean, the most interesting thing to do there is stalk the blogs of people who live in places interesting enough that they, in turn, can stalk celebrities. But I have my one friend and my enabling parents and the knowledge of where they store alcohol and I'm not ready to stop being seventeen. So. There."

A beat. Out of the corner of my eye, I see Ash turn to me slowly.

"Jules. Are you comparing my fall from grace and my consequent eternal punishment as one of the damned to the fact that you're nervous about going to college?"

"No. I just want you to know something personal and embarrassing about me 'cause you shared something about yourself before. The fall and Lucifer and all that. Didn't seem fair."

"I already know enough embarrassing information about you."

"Really?"

I catch him nodding out of the corner of my eye and wonder if his knowing about me is a newly demonic or a formerly angelic thing. Seems best not to speculate. Apparently that's something he's sensitive about. But still . . .

"Why did you fall?" I ask for the second time, trying to come across as nonchalant. It's a good thing I have the excuse of staring out the windshield to avoid looking at his reaction, as I'm sure none of this is as touching coming from a girl who looks like she got her head stuck in a food processor. In the distance is a yellow dinosaur with what appears to be people gathered around it. The dinosaur's tail and jaw are moving slowly, mechanically. Ash doesn't deny me right away, instead he takes his time answering my question.

"I was on Earth duty. I'm not certain how long ago, but Lady Gaga was in a dress made of meat and there was a Harry Potter film coming out. Those were the two things everyone was talking about. I'd only been allowed to actually watch over Earth for a short time at that point. Always stuck up in Heaven before my promotion. I was curious and I made a bad decision. When my time came to go back to Heaven, I found my feet getting sucked down into the ground below instead. And I just kept sinking. So here I am now, in Hell."

"You made a bad decision?"

"Yes."

I don't press any more. I suppose I've already learned more about secret biblical matters than most humans my age. Hell blurs by outside the windows and driving doesn't even feel real anymore. Nothing does. Why should it? I have had dreams more realistic than this.

A graveyard comes into view on our left and Ash says, "We're here."

"But you said—"

"The hospital is behind the graveyard."

Hand over hand, I turn the wheel violently so we half skid off the road, through mud that splatters onto the windshield and has no right to exist somewhere so arid, and towards the headstones.

"You know, I think it's about time I made a bad decision myself," I mutter.

"What are you . . ."

Ash trails off as I undo my seatbelt—which is a ridiculous thing to still be wearing—and reach into the backseat, my knees in the driver's seat and my torso flung over the center console. After a few moments, I return victorious, holding my switchblade in the air.

"My arm is complete again!" I announce proudly, and the confused expression on Ash's face lets me know two things: One—he has never seen *Sweeney Todd* which, for a demon, is a downright shame. And, two—he thinks I've cracked and gone completely insane.

To be fair, there's a decent amount of evidence to support the correctness of that second item. Recently, summoning a demon. Before that, getting into a fistfight at lunch over whether or not Fletcher Fatale is tragically in love with his arch-nemesis. Spoiler alert: he is. But that's a completely different matter.

I press the button on the knife and watch it swing open, promptly ignore my blood crusted on the blade, and hold it out to Ash. He stares at the knife in total bewilderment.

"What—"

"Take it," I urge, and he complies after a moment, holding out his hand. "Come on."

I get out of the car and walk towards the headstones; he was right, there's a hospital in the distance. Ash's door opens and shuts and mushy footsteps follow. This isn't a breakdown. This is reasonable, considering the circumstances. There's a perfectly lovely headstone, about knee-high and belonging to a Dora Lynne Rogers, which I sit on. Ash isn't very far behind, of course. For a second, I wonder if we should take this opportunity to test the exact distance apart from one another he can stand, but decide against it. Doesn't seem like something Ash will really go for. No. It's best we stick together as if we like one another.

There's a demon stalking towards me with a bloody knife in a graveyard and I beckon him forward.

"I need you to cut the rest of my hair."

"With this knife?" he asks slowly. I shrug.

"You left those scissors lodged in that not-so-nice woman's neck and this is all I have in terms of sharp cutty things."

"Are you sure you don't want your hair anymore?" he asks again, weirdly shaken.

"What's the point? What's left is a wreck. Get rid of it." Maybe it's foolish of me to trust him. Actually, there's no *maybe* about it. This is foolish. But he held my hand and he's killed for me already.

"How short?" He inches slightly closer, and I have to tilt my head up further to look at him. And I really look.

"As short as yours."

He raises an eyebrow and runs a hand over his nearly nonexistent hair, but knows better than to ask again.

"This isn't going to work if you want your hair to look like mine," he says, holding up the knife. "But if you trust me, I might be able to manage it another way."

A beat. I nod. It would be impossible not to trust him at this point and besides, his job training was in being an angel of the Lord. Well, I assume it's "of the Lord."

He nods back, something small and jerky while sticking the knife in his back pocket, then reaches out and covers my head with both his hands. He must feel me flinch because he pulls back for a moment, then returns them. A tingling spreads out over my scalp, which is startling at first but then begins to feel oddly nice. Like when spicy food makes your lips go all fuzzy. The feeling passes after a few seconds and he removes his hands, takes a step back, and coughs nervously.

I run my fingers through my hair. False.

I run my fingers over the peach fuzz that now adorns my head and wish it made me feel something. Some sort of loss. But I guess this makes as much sense as Marcus dying: none at all.

"Thank you."

"No problem," Ash responds. "You may have stolen most of my powers but this was barely demonic. It's nice to be able to do something extraordinary, even if it's only giving you a magic haircut."

It's so easy to ignore, or even forget, the extent of what I've done to him.

"How does this work? Having your powers bound and all that? You were able to open the entryway, and now you've done this."

He shrugs as I shake my head from side to side, getting used to hair not flying around with each movement.

"I've never fully understood demonic abilities, what we can and cannot do, but when I change reality I'm not doing a little trick. I'm looking at the matter that makes up the universe, picking apart what it's composed of, and reforming it how I like. The major distinction in terms of demonic power versus angelic is having malicious intent. Maybe my impulse decisions are slipping out like magical sneezes. Or maybe my reasoning behind doing certain things isn't evil enough."

He doesn't wish evil on me. He should, but he doesn't.

"Thank you, Ashmodai," I repeat, and with those words I suddenly feel as if I'm about to cry, except it's not because of the hair. Tears begin slipping out against my will.

There is nothing worse than being seventeen.

What the Hell am I doing?

The Hell. Hell.

My brain is television static and barely thought-out sentences. I can't breathe properly but that also doesn't seem to matter here.

In Hell.

Why did I ever think this was a good idea?

"I can make it grow back!" Ash shouts, breaking through my reverie of panic and hormones.

"It's not the hair that's making me upset." I look up. He extends an arm, as if he's about to put a hand on my shoulder, then drops it.

"I didn't hurt you, did I?"

"No, not at all." I offer him a weak and undoubtedly watery smile as my breathing returns to normal, although I can't seem to convince the tears to stop pouring out of my eyes. But then I realize how considerate he's being. For some reason, he seems worried about causing me pain even though all I've been doing is cause *him* pain. The sobs begin again.

The tragic part of all this is that I'm probably just tired and hungry. I hate crying like this, when it's noisy, unstoppable, and over something stupid. I once had a breakdown over not being able to flip a crepe properly. Ugh. I can't wait to have a fully developed brain.

"What's wrong now?" he asks, looking uncomfortable enough to crawl out of his own skin.

"Laura isn't coming to John Jay with me and no one's gonna want to talk to me because the only thing I wanna talk about is Marcus."

The words don't feel intelligible as I say them through pathetic, gasp-like sobs, but Ash seems to understand regardless.

"That's definitely not what I was expecting," he says after a moment, then goes to lean against a neighboring headstone. "Look, you're going to college. Make new friends."

He speaks as if it's that easy, making friends, and I glare. "What are you going to college for again?" he asks.

"I want to be a lawyer. You can't do that straight out of high school, though, so I'm getting my undergrad degree in anthropology before law school."

He lifts an eyebrow at "anthropology" but then says, "Well, there you go! I'm sure lawyers have tons of friends. Don't they have a lot of money?"

"Yeah, and a lot of enemies, too."

The reason I want to study law and know I'll be good at it is *because* I'm so unpleasant. I'm always willing to fight, and sometimes I start arguments out of boredom. In middle school, people used to wind me up and set me loose. They would feed me gossip about their friends and enemies, then encourage me to confront them about it. That's probably why I had so few friends before Laura and none other than her, now. Which is almost impressive considering I'm attractive enough *and* own a car.

I don't want to be alone.

I do not want to be alone.

I'm good at taking sides and arguing for that side. I'm going to be a great paralegal and an amazing first-year associate, and then after that, a wonderful lawyer. But I don't anticipate having many friends. I try to find other interests and hobbies but nothing sticks. I'm mediocre at pretty much everything and nothing is fun enough to keep trying. All I have is my tenacity and even I know that's bullshit.

I open my mouth to tell Ash exactly that and am promptly cut off by an ear-splitting scream, the likes of which I've only heard in horror films. Screams of this nature are much worse when not coming out of crappy TV speakers. I throw my hands over my ears and fall off the headstone. As if the mess in my head couldn't get any worse.

Another scream. Another.

"Stymphalian birds!" Ash shouts.

He's pointing overhead and I look up to see a metallic, copper-colored mass heading our way. The flock pulsates and beats as the noise grows increasingly loud.

Ash grabs me by the arm, pulls me upright, and whispers, "Run."

The idiot begins running towards the birds, dragging me along. I don't know what they do but have enough context clues to figure out it probably isn't pretty. I try to drag him in the opposite direction but continue getting pulled along the way he wants to go.

"We should head back to the car," I shout, trying to will my still-gelatinous legs to keep up with his annoyingly steady ones. Ash either genuinely doesn't hear over the mechanical flap of wings and unholy screeching, or he pretends not to. His destination is obvious: the hospital in the distance. If we had a moment to discuss this, I'd probably say something along the lines of, "Hey, it's great that you're so focused on getting us to the hospital, but wouldn't it be best to not run directly beneath some monsters towards a frankly frightening building behind a graveyard when there is a delightfully familiar car only a few feet away?"

Best not to fantasize about these things, though. Instead, I run.

For a second, I wonder why they would ever need a graveyard in the afterlife, but then I shake my head and focus solely on the feeling of my feet pounding against the ground.

We weave around gravestones and jump over tricky roots of dead trees with surprising ease. The two of us really need to stop holding hands like this, people might get the wrong idea. I want to laugh. And cry. And take a shot of tequila. Instead, I keep moving.

Ash squeezes my arm right before we dart directly underneath the cloud of birds as if to say *To battle!* and then there's no escaping them. The hospital is close, but the creatures are closer.

"Holy shit!" I scream when something sharp and horrible lodges itself into the ground next to me. It appears to be a car part or space junk jutting out of the dirt.

More metallic shards begin to rain down and without speaking, Ash continues to lead us towards the building. The area in front of the hospital has an overhanging ledge, like where ambulances would pull up, except no roads lead to it. Without thinking, because there's definitely not enough room in my brain for that right now, I fling myself bodily towards the building and roll under the overhang, dragging Ash with me. Of course, flinging oneself from some nice dirt onto a cement floor is not the best way to prevent scraped knees. And elbows. And limbs. And heads.

I lie there for a hot second, savoring the sound of flapping wings overhead and the knowledge that they can't get me. The screams are no match for the throbbing in my thoroughly shaken head.

"What the fuck, Jules?" Ash says.

"Got us out of the way."

"I was in the process of doing that already, if you hadn't noticed, and my method involved us covered in much less of our own blood!"

"Those birds—" I begin asking. He stops me right away.

"They're gone. Not the brightest creatures. What they can't see doesn't exist."

"Like babies," I wheeze, trying to catch my breath. "What did you call them before?"

"Stymphalian birds. Nasty. I had a bit of a bad encounter with them when I first arrived. They shit poison, have metal feathers to launch at their enemies, and scream like a bunch of motherfuckers. Not to mention they used to be women."

"Really? Human women?"

"Yep. It's pretty safe to assume that everything here is a punishment for someone who used to be on Earth. I'm not sure what the process of turning a dead lady into a metal bird looks like, but I'm certain it isn't pretty."

I shiver at the thought. And then I continue shivering because it's cold and I'm pretty sure my blood isn't flowing in the proper directions.

"We need to keep going," I say.

We stand side by side and look at the automatic glass doors standing between us and a sterile-looking white room. Counters gleam in the distance. While the theme park and graveyard took me by surprise, I have no questions about what a hospital is doing in Hell. They are some of the creepiest places I can imagine, and I'm sure they've seen more pain than the rest of the world combined.

Rate your pain on a scale of one to ten, I think. *Rate your pain.*

"Shall we?" Ash says, holding out his arm. I link mine through his, pretending like we're characters in that cute period piece Marcus starred in when he was twenty. Anything to push the memories from my last visit to a hospital from my mind.

"We shall."

The doors slide open and the waiting room seems like a typical one, with uncomfortable-looking chairs that have padding everywhere except the armrests and a tile floor that wants to seem marbled but instead looks diseased. Fitting.

And empty.

We walk past the front desk, through a set of huge double doors into a hallway that would usually lead to patient rooms but here could lead to any number of horrible places. I lean in slightly closer to Ash.

"Where do they keep the computers?" he asks, his words and posture guarded, as if he's expecting an attack at any moment.

"The nurses' stations."

They're probably in other places too, but I know that one for certain. They used to make these poor volunteers take me for walks down the hallway and we would always pass the nurses' station where scrub-wearing women tapped away on outdated keyboards all day long.

Each step we take reverberates through the empty halls, and no matter how many times I look over my shoulder and see nothing, it's impossible to shake the feeling we're being followed. As we move farther in, the hospital looks less and less like the one I stayed in. It looks impossibly older, with giant metal light fixtures hanging bowl-like overhead and a checkerboard tile floor. Farther down the hallway, doors line the walls, spread uneven distances from one another and numbered according to a system I can't even begin to comprehend. I release Ash's arm, go up to one labeled 292, and turn its large, brass handle.

Inside, there's a man screaming on a metal bed, breaking the absolute silence of the hall. Strapped down and fighting against his restraints, he's arched upwards and contorted in a way that can only mean extreme amounts of pain. There's something wrong with his skin. I slam the door shut as quickly as I opened it. Ash is expressionless. I doubt the same can be said of myself, but I try to appear similarly stoic as I walk over to the next door. Number 73.

I brace myself, both mentally and physically, before pushing the door open and finding another man strapped to another bed, this one whimpering like he's been through so much agony that he has no more screams to offer. There's an irregular pattern of dripping sounds resonating through the room—maybe they were also present in the last one—as if to not let whoever this is forget where they are.

An arm appears to be protruding from the wrong part of his body. To be precise, where his left leg should be. I slam the door shut.

"Who are these people?"

"A variety of unfortunates. Mainly doctors who used to perform medical experiments on others, which is a fancy way of saying they were torturers."

My face must fall considerably because he tacks on, "We're in Hell, honey. Most of the people here deserve it. Did you honestly think that some metal birds would be the worst of the monsters?"

I shake my head, wondering how much Ash really thinks that everyone down here deserves it, and he offers to open the next door for me. And the one after that. And the one after that. I'm hoping there will be a computer of some sort in one of these rooms, even though everything seems a bit too old-fashioned for that, but instead the sights are all similarly grisly and completely unhelpful. I stop processing them. Empty eye sockets. Melting flesh. We reach the double doors at the end of the hall and he flings them open to reveal a child: a little girl in a frilly dress, with curly blonde hair and rosy cheeks, like she belongs in an advertisement from the 1950s.

She looks up at us and smiles.

"Close the door," I state as calmly as possible, but Ash is already ahead of me and pulling it shut.

Except a tiny shoe gets in the way. A tiny shoe, attached to a tiny leg, attached to the girl who moves quicker than should be possible. She pries the door back, pulling the handle directly out of Ash's hand.

"Are you here to help me?" she asks.

I reach for the handle but she flings the door wide open and takes a step forward, feet planted firmly on the linoleum floors in front of us, so clean they reflect a mirror image of her small form.

"Are you here to help me?" she repeats. "You found me so you must be here to help me."

Ash sputters through the beginning of at least ten different sentences like he's speaking in tongues. Every step we take backward, this child matches with one forward. Thrilling to see where horror films must get their inspiration from.

"Do you," I begin saying, but then lose my voice due to the complete and utter terror. I try again. "Do you know where the nurses' station is?"

"Is that who you're looking for? A nurse?" she asks, and I watch her body slowly begin to morph.

Is no one down here constrained by their shape?

Who am I kidding? It's Hell. Of course they aren't. Her legs grow longer, but not to the extent of the Fate, and her clothing transforms until standing a head taller than me, and perfectly eye-level with Ash, is a nurse. An uncomfortably, stereotypically "sexy" nurse in a white dress and hat, like something from a low-budget movie, and if my heart hadn't stopped at the sight of the blood- and rust-stained clothing, I would have some undeniably witty quip about Hell being the perfect place for gender stereotypes like this one.

Except I'm pretty sure she has syringes for fingers now. That's not something witty quips survive.

"Valac," Ash says, backing up until we hit a wall. "We're coworkers but we haven't met before."

He holds up a trembling hand as if to shake Valac's, but then notes the needle fingers and sensibly drops it back to his side.

"No, Ashmodai, we haven't."

Valac strokes the side of Ash's face with the sharp point of one of the needles, pressing it ever so slightly into his cheek. A drop of blood oozes out and crawls a slow path down Ash's neck, like a single tear.

I have the stupidest idea in all of recorded history.

With all the feeble strength contained within my noodle arms and upper body, I shove Valac as hard as possible. Which isn't very hard at all, but it manages to throw the demon slightly off balance. Until Valac reaches out to steady herself and plunges five syringes deep into the meaty lower half of my left arm.

A scream. A split-second decision. I run, yanking my arm desperately and feeling the needles drag through my flesh. Delicate blue veins bursting open, being sliced clean through. It is over instantaneously and I don't look down.

Do. Not. Look. Down. I pull the knife out of Ash's back pocket. Fletcher Fatale has gone through worse.

Fletcher Fatale watched his family get murdered in front of him. He climbed frosty mountains and starved for months, all for the sake of justice. He's been stabbed and burned and punched.

I run to the room with the whimpering man and burst inside. No time to think. Fletcher Fatale certainly wouldn't. I slice straight through the man's restraints, legs first, then arms, and drag him off the cot. He's a greasy man who I push towards the door before running out myself and going to the next room over. No time to see or hear. Barely any time to bleed.

Same thing. *Slice. Slice. Slice. Slice. Up. Shove. Out.* And again. And again.

And I finally run out into the hall with my knife held high, ready to shove it into the neck of anyone who tries to fuck with me, but see that my work is being done for me. I'd say "exactly as planned," but it wasn't a plan so much as internalized screaming on a loop that resulted in action. I slip the knife into my back pocket.

The patients—deformed, sewn together, limbs lopped and reattached in a variety of truly awful patterns—are on top of Valac. I have never before seen the actions of people who truly have nothing left to lose, especially not people well versed in the ways of enacting untold evil on others.

Ash is plastered against the wall, arms spread out with hands clinging to the bricks like he's about to crawl up it backwards, watching the gruesome display.

"*Ash!*" I shout, and his head snaps towards me instantly, stricken eyes wide open.

I waggle my arms as if to say *Come now! Come quick, you absolute idiot.* He gets the hint and inches sideways until he is out of the way, and then stumbles over to me.

"Let's go," I say and he nods.

For once, neither of us feel compelled to run, which is a small mercy because I'm starting to realize how screwed up my body feels. The hallway starts to warp around me as we walk. I stagger to a wall and slump against it. *Oh no. Not again.*

How goddamn typical of me.

"Jules?" Ash asks.

"I don't . . . I don't . . ."

Walls tilt. Floors twist.

And then, everything is black.

> *I'm in a garden and Elle is there. Elle, Anita, and Laura. They're all so beautiful.*
> *I love them.*
> *"Hello," they say to me, all in unison. I smile.*
> *"Hello."*

CHAPTER FIVE

In which Cher and statistics
become purveyors of untruths.

Dear Marcus,

I read that interview the other day, the one where you say how shocked you are to be the sexiest man alive. You also say a few other unfairly disparaging things. Marcus, that isn't right. You are the sexiest man alive and it only takes a mirror to prove it. I have enclosed a handheld one with this letter, just in case. I'm a teenage girl from New Jersey with more hormones than I know what to do with, so if anyone should be self-conscious, it's me. Let's make a deal: I'll hate myself twice as much as I already do and in exchange, you won't dislike anything about yourself at all.

xxx,
Julia R. Tolliver

Black.

No, not black. Emptiness. A voice.

"Jules? Open your eyes. Please. At least open your mouth. Come on, Jules. I can't believe you're doing this to me again."

A man? That's not Laura. Laura's usually there when this happens. Or my mother. Female voices in my head. Lovely. That's not a female, that's Ash.

Like a vacuum is turned on in my memory, everything that just took place gets sucked back into my brain and my eyes fly open.

"Calm down," I say, my mouth not working quite as well as I'd like. "I'm not choking on anything."

I sit up with some assistance from Ash, who is crouched next to me looking endearingly perplexed. Endearingly? *Ew.*

"Is this a regular thing for you?" he asks. He sounds angry at me, which is extremely unfair.

"Yes, actually, but I'd like to see *you* stay conscious after having all that happen to you."

I wave my right arm around to indicate the pool of blood that is slowly dripping out of my other arm and onto the floor around me. So much for not staining my cute, white shorts.

"Let's keep going," I say, moving to get up, but he puts a hand on my shoulder and keeps me sitting.

"Are you sure you feel well enough?" he asks. "I don't like seeing you on the ground like that."

"Yeah, well, I don't particularly enjoy being down here," I say, getting up and cursing my body for being broken. Only enough to be an inconvenience, but not enough to get any exploitable amount of pity. "Come on, we've got to get moving. I'll find some bandages and be loads better after."

We continue walking, me trying to ignore the pain emanating from my arm as it drips a dismal trail behind us. The nurses' station isn't far.

"If you were on Earth, I imagine this would be the ideal place to pass out," Ash says. "But we aren't on Earth so the opposite is probably true."

"Look at all of these bandages though," I say, trying to look on the bright side, as dull as it is. There are bandages galore strewn over various shelves, disorderly but clean. I grab a roll and begin wrapping it around my arm. The first layer turns red immediately, so I keep going until my arm is three times the size it was previously.

It's a miracle that I'm not someone who passes out at the sight of blood, or else I'd be spending a lot more time unconscious during this trip. Ash watches me work, doing nothing to help whatsoever, until something behind the faux-wooden counter catches his eye.

"A computer!"

He hops over the top of the counter, swinging his legs and scooching his ass to get to the other side.

"You know you could walk around it," I point out while doing exactly that.

He shrugs and holds an ancient white MacBook high above his head with both hands. It's as thick as three of my laptops, but does appear to have a USB drive which is a considerable advantage. Mine at home is too sleek to have any useful inputs. I smile as he hands it to me.

"Let's get out of here."

Ash keeps his eyes on me as we exit the building. Thinking about that makes me think about the pointed looks that Fletcher Fatale would give Ferdinand Ferdinand, which makes me think about Laura and me doing a shot whenever one would happen on screen during our sleepovers. The first time I tried alcohol was with Laura—she's a messy drunk—and almost every time I've had it since has been with her as well.

I miss it. Being drunk with Laura. Her explaining the plot of a movie in long, slipping syllables or tipsy singing as we walk down the street.

All this to say, I do everything in my power to avoid thinking about hospitals. It doesn't take too long to find our way out. Actually, it's alarmingly easy, suspiciously so, considering all the twists and turns through random halls we had to make on our quest for the computer. Ash seems worried, and I assume he's thinking something similar. We make it to the front lobby, out the sliding glass doors, and back to the graveyard. Sulfurous air has never felt so good.

Once we get to the car, I barely sit down before powering the computer on, one-handed.

"Do you want to try and find somewhere to rest first?" Ash offers.

I ignore him in favor of watching the screen come to life, dark grey and slow to load.

"Did you hear me?" he tries again. "You're human. You probably need to sleep so you don't pass out again. Or crash into any trees, for that matter."

"I'm not tired."

"But—"

"I'm not tired. We need to keep moving. Haven't you figured it out yet? This world is trying to kill us! Between The Fates and the birds and that creepy nurse child, we're obviously under attack."

"Or we're just in Hell," Ash shoots back. "Why do you think I spend all my days locked in a diner with the most annoying demon imaginable? Down here, everyone *is always under attack.*"

"All the more reason to not stop."

The bottom of the laptop is dangerously hot against my legs. A flashing green text cursor appears and invites me to type, but I simply insert the flash drive and wait. A box pops up with a single folder labeled the same as the side of the memory stick: "The Damned—Alphabetically and Regionally." I click on it.

"Oh, thank God," I say.

"You really shouldn't," Ash responds, and it's easy to see that he's still feeling pissy.

"There's a search box. I think we can type in names like this," my fingers fly across the keys in a pattern more familiar than my own name, "and *voila!* Marcus is at a place called Marbas' Crisis in Dolus. Number 492-669."

"Those numbers don't mean anything, coming up with them is someone else's punishment. Dolus, though. That's interesting."

"Is it far?"

"Depends on how Hell is feeling. Usually it isn't too far, though. The major cities of Hell are close enough, and it's a section of one of those."

I hand the laptop to Ash and start up the car, glancing appreciatively at the gas gauge that still thinks we have a full tank.

"Does it mean something? That he's in Dolus?"

"What?"

"Like Dante. We read him last year. Every section of Hell was reserved for a different type of sinner. What does Dolus mean?"

"Nothing you should worry about right now. I'm just happy we know so I can focus on getting you to him and getting my old life back."

"You want your old life back?"

"My old life didn't include little girls who don't know what's best for them."

I drive with one hand on the wheel and the other throbbing in my lap, the bandages looking worse for wear. The skies of Hell are almost beautiful now, an otherworldly mix of hues, like someone gave up halfway through painting the sky and threw the rest of the shades up there. A Jackson Pollock made of light.

"Huh," Ash murmurs.

"What is it?"

"This computer is sentient. Its name is Dorian."

I see that he has it open in his lap, grab the computer from him, leaving no hands on the wheel, and toss it into the backseat.

"I didn't say it was an evil computer!" he shouts, looking deliciously affronted.

"You didn't say it was a good one, either. We're not taking any chances with stupid, demonic computers. No way."

He grumbles a bit, so I decide to risk turning on the radio instead of my podcast, hoping this will show how open-minded and amenable I am. Against all odds, Cher is singing.

"Is this—"

"'I Got You Babe?'" Ash fills in. "Yep." He pops his lips on the *P* sound. "Sonny really made an impact down here."

"Huh," I respond noncommittally, not wanting to admit I have no idea who Sonny is.

We drive for a long time. Or maybe we drive for no time at all. Honestly, it's a very common problem I've come across during our road trip through Hell. One thing is certain: this station is playing more songs than "I Got You Babe," but by the sixth time we hear it we're both singing along word-for-word to the entire thing. We drive past beaten-down shacks and gas stations that don't look like they've ever seen petrol, let alone have the capacity to sell it, as well as tall, gleaming office buildings with windows so clean they reflect the light blindingly into the road, making the air inside the car physically warm when we drive through the beams of brightness.

Screw open-mindedness. I grab another CD and switch to the podcast.

> Welcome, welcome, welcome everyone! You may remember me putting out a general call for catchphrases and theme songs, and while none of you submitted anything worthwhile, I must say that I'm in love with the logo that was posted on our page the other day. Whoever has the username 'thoughtsofthots' designed this wonderful image of Absinthe as a Transformer-type robot. Miss Thot's explanation for this is that the acronym of Rich Bitch On the Run is R.B.O.T.R., which sort of looks like the word *robot*. I'll go along with that. Congratulations on officially making this podcast robot themed. Now one of you needs to think of a theme song and soon we'll be on the way to seeming like a legitimate artistic venture.

Anyway, back to the trip. Anita and I took a wrong turn down Zzyzx Road—please google the spelling of that—and ended up in the Mojave Desert. White expanses stretched out into the heat-wave horizon with these boulders embedded in the ground. I stood in that dry heat and reveled in how vast and flat everything was. Dirt roads and dreams and all that clichéd crap. As we tried to find our way back to the interstate or whatever major road we were on, a car pulled up next to us to tell us that our gas tank was open. It's strange. They seemed friendly enough, but Anita and I were both scared to death.

This was only exacerbated later on when we passed a blackened shell of a car on the side of the road, smoldering and smoking. A car fire. I stuck my head out of the sunroof to see and understood why the area we passed through before was called Death Valley.

We stayed in another hostel in Vegas. Signs inside warned against entering both the strip club and tattoo parlor, on either side of the building. There were more drive-in chapels across the street than there could ever be couples enough to fill them. We took one of the free maps and circled everything that two girls under the age of twenty-one could do and the quickest route between all of our prospective destinations. We weren't planning to stay long because one of the receptionists seemed like a bit of a creep, and I had a strong suspicion he knew who I was. He offered to do my laundry for free and it sounded more like an invitation into his bed.

At the first casino we went to, there were massive fountains and flowers arranged to look like European cities. The next one had an Eiffel Tower, which I preferred to the real one. We went on a looping roller coaster ride through the streets of New York City and ate sushi in a place where the waitstaff inexplicably began performing intricately choreographed dance routines. The next day really did prove that the entire world exists in Vegas, considering we ate breakfast in Paris then walked down a street in Italy. We got conned into sitting at one of those oxygen bars. You know, where they shove cannulas up your nose and argue that it's meant to make you feel revitalized. The woman working there told us all the celebrities were doing it and I was like, well now I have to.

After feeling no change at the oxygen bar, we walked the strip for quite some time. Saw an Elvis impersonator driving a pink convertible and loving his life as another person.

That night at the hostel, when I was alone, the receptionist boy tried something. What made it worse is that he cushioned his crude come-ons with all these stories about illnesses I don't believe he actually has, and how his struggle will help him become a famous screenwriter. He called me one of the most badass people he had ever met.

The text he sent me that night, and lord knows how he got my number, was one of the worst things I have ever read and I still have it saved in case I ever need blackmail material.

We played "Viva Las Vegas" on the drive out of the city.

CHAPTER SIX

**In which a well is discussed
and a demon is ensnared.**

Dear Marcus,

*I really hate young adult literature. And I'm
not saying this to be different and cool, I genuinely
have a foolproof argument for why it's the worst:
the drunk older sister. No matter what book I
read, the main (female) character always has a
slightly older sister who wears revealing clothes
and gets drunk and parties. She's inevitably judged
throughout the entire book, villainized for not being
a basic judgmental bitch, and is usually allowed a
redemption arc that consists of her giving it all up
and basically turning into a nun like her bookish
younger sister. Bleh. I don't see what's so bad about
parties and alcohol. This is why young people don't
want to read, not because we're stupid.*

*I saw an interview the other day where you
said your favorite book is* The Catcher in the Rye.
*Is that true? I like to pretend that you actually
lie around reading trashy romance novels in your*

spare time. Don't worry, your secret is safe with me.
Regardless, I'll do my best to enjoy The Catcher in
the Rye *when we get to it this term, but I make no*
promises. Books just aren't my thing.

With love and everything that goes along with it,
Julia R. Tolliver

We drive past buildings that look like posh Floridian condos. I
ask Ash what's inside.

"Nothing good."

"How do you know?"

"I just do."

"I don't know, sounds fake to me."

I'm pressing his buttons on purpose. No idea why. Maybe
it's a manifestation of me wanting to get Marcus and get the hell
out. No pun intended.

"Look, when I became a demon and found myself
delightfully damned for the rest of my days—"

"Nice alliteration."

"Thank you. Anyway, when I fell from favor with the people
up there, I found myself sucked directly into Hell with a whole
bunch of information pertinent to being a demon dropped into
my head and no instruction on how to use it. So, what am I
supposed to do? I was trained to be an angel, I know all the rules
of being a demon, but no one thought to come and tell me how
to reconcile these two things. All this to say, I know this area isn't
safe. I can hardly tell a hawk from a handsaw here."

"Fair enough."

There is a bump in the road. Another. A third.

There's been a bump in the conversation, as well.

"When I was a kid," I begin saying, words flowing out of me
like vomit. Like I'm not still a kid. Like if I begin to share more
of myself with Ash, he'll continue to do the same in return. "I
had this book of New Jersey folklore. There was a story about
a road with seven bumps on it, and the reason they were there

was because there were seven witches buried underneath. They'd been hanged on a tree to the side of the road, which of course hadn't been a road back in those times. I'm assuming. Eventually cars were invented and roads got paved and no matter how many times the road was paved over, and how smooth they got it, the next day there would be seven more bumps."

"Spooky," Ash says, like this tangent was completely expected and perfectly normal.

"I know, right? I thought it was fantastic."

"I'm sorry to say that what we ran over probably wasn't witch bodies. They're on the total opposite end of Hell."

"Witches are real?"

"You launched a bunch of evil ex-doctors at a shape-shifting monster child with needle fingers and you're acting shocked that witches exist?"

"*Touché.*"

"'More' things in heaven and 'earth'—"

"'Than are dreamt of in your philosophy?'" I finish. "You know Shakespeare?"

"Not personally. You?"

"No. But we covered *Hamlet* and *Julius Caesar* in school. Plus, he's Elle's favorite author; she's got him tattooed on her thigh. That got me to pay some more attention in class. I find it all a bit stabby for my taste, though. Preferred *Frankenstein*."

"That's less stabby?"

"Not really. But it's the most interesting thing you read in school. I'm convinced the majority of the books they let us learn about are propaganda by adults to convince teenagers to not have any fun."

"I can't really say, considering I've never been to high school."

"Lucky you."

Ash sits there for a moment, seemingly pondering our conversation, then says, "You're really into this Elle person, aren't you?"

It sounds like he's implying something that I'm not quite grasping.

"Yes. I really am," I answer, knowing it's impossible to express how much she means to me in words. He doesn't know me well enough to get it. Laura doesn't even fully understand the extent of my adoration for Elle Dixon, and how it goes beyond her last name, and Laura has known me since before it all began.

Elle was once on a panel of female artists, and she definitely didn't belong with them. She became news after announcing, drunkenly, at one of their speaking engagements that she was a virgin. This was in response to someone asking her about her sexuality during a Q and A portion. She said that she knew she wasn't straight, but no other labels felt cozy. They didn't fit right.

That's when she stood up and shouted, "I'm a virgin!" and then proclaimed that maybe if someone slept with her, she'd have an easier time figuring it all out and that she would be accepting applications from potential suitors of all genders for the rest of the day.

What happened after that isn't clear, but she announced on social media the next day that she was: no longer a virgin; sorry to anyone who thought she was implying that they had to have sex to know their own sexuality; ten vodka shots deep during the panel; and queer.

The word was comfortable enough and no further definition was required.

Some fans called it a ploy to get laid, saying she couldn't possibly have been a virgin. Others called it a commendable stunt to reclaim the word *queer* and destigmatize virginity. I called it the most fascinating thing I'd ever seen.

"Look to your left," Ash says, and I glance out the window, shaking myself out of these thoughts of Elle. There's a massive ditch on the side of the road with a sign in front of it that I don't manage to read by the time we zoom past.

"What's that, then?"

"The Well to Hell."

"We're already in Hell," I point out.

"Yeah, I think it's someone's poor attempt at being funny. There was a hoax on Earth saying that these construction workers in Europe drilled so deep that they hit Hell and found proof of its existence. This somehow got to America, where religious radio stations began playing audio of screams they claimed to have recorded in the well they were drilling. Someone thought it was the most hilarious thing that the humans had done yet and demanded our own Well to Hell, so it sits down here. Sometimes you can even hear screams."

"Did you learn all that when they dumped the Hell info into your head? Like you mentioned before?" I ask.

Ash actually laughs at that.

"No. I once sat next to one of its architects at the diner."

"Huh." Deep breath. "Thank you for telling me."

It almost feels like I'm bonding with my new demon friend, like he doesn't mind being bound to me and dragged across Hell to rescue a middle-aged Brit. I don't want it to stop, to scare him back into putting on that moderately douchey shell. I know he wants to talk about deep things. Sleepover things. Girls-with-their-friends things.

"Well, you're not the only one with stories," he says, smiling.

The streets are starting to look more familiar, like the main roads running through New Jersey. My mother used to say that New Jersey roads are the most beautiful in the world because of all the trees. That can't possibly be true, but then again, she has said a lot of things that aren't true. Like when she tells her friends how perfectly healthy and totally fine I am. How delightfully normal. All this is running through my head, not as a nice parade of thoughts one after another but instead some weird tumor of sporadic memories, when we pass a sign for an upcoming rest stop. Ash jerks upright next to me.

"Pull over," he says, an undercurrent of tension in his voice.

"Why?"

"Just pull over."

"Into the rest stop?" I ask, glancing over.

There's something off about his eyes. I've seen this before with Laura when she used to have manic episodes. Now she has meds for that and we don't talk about it. I have a feeling Ash does not have meds for whatever this is. I've been through this enough to know to listen, though, and head where he asks.

The parking lot is a parking lot. The rest stop is a rest stop. It looks like one that would be named after a morally dubious founding father. I pull into a space a few rows back from the entrance. By the time I have the car in park, Ash is out and walking away. When did he even unbuckle his seat belt? It takes a moment for my brain to catch up, and I am out of the car even quicker.

"Where are you going?" I shout as he walks to the door. He ignores me. I run over the pavement and grab him by the shoulder.

"Ash, listen to me!"

He shakes off my hand and turns, eyes glazed over and teeth bared.

"I can hear him," he says and continues walking.

Once, when I was a small child, my dad set a trap in the backyard. I'm not certain what it was meant for, but he caught a possum instead. I remember sneaking out to look at it, all matted fur and hisses through yellow teeth. Dead, black eyes and a putrid tail. It was trapped, and it had no goodness left in it. It led to one of the first arguments I ever had with my parents. A long, nasty one.

Ash looks like that poor possum. Feral. For the first time, he looks like a demon, and I hate it. My insides feel like they're contracting.

"Who?" I ask as I take a few steps forward and wrap my arms around his waist, hoping to snap him out of whatever is happening. "Stop and talk to me."

"No." Ash pries me off. "I can hear him."

I reach for Ash again but he catches my hand and pushes me back. A sudden shock of pain. A burning across my cheek and I'm folded over.

The bastard slapped me. There is *no* way that's going to fly this time, even if he has no upper body strength to speak of. Something is wrong. He would never go this far away from me considering our bond; he's terrified of that pain. By the time I've gathered myself, I see the door to the rest stop swinging shut and know he's gone in.

I rush after him. Inside, there are dozens of people, all dressed abysmally and mopping at a snail's pace. I pay them no mind because Ash is walking across the checkered linoleum floor to a figure on the other side, not a mopper but a large silhouette shrouded in shadow. I try to run but slip and land on my ass.

Ash walks too far for our bond to handle. From the ground, I see the exact moment when he inhales sharply then cries out, falling to his knees.

"Ash!" I shout.

He turns his head towards me and whimpers. "Jules?"

I can hardly make out the word because of our distance. Before I can move, the shadow is on him and Ash is gone.

"Ash," I say. And then I repeat his name, louder and louder. I stand upright and run to where he was just standing, sliding on the damp floors but not losing my footing. *Nothing.* I wave my arms around, hoping he's turned invisible or something, but I don't strike anything solid. *Nope.* I run around like a madman, dodging everyone. Like the Devil is on my tail. Like Fletcher Fatale when he's being chased by Ferdinand Ferdinand, even though I know he's secretly hoping to be caught. The gift shop, the fast food restaurants, even the bathrooms are full of dull-eyed people in blue jumpsuits, no demons in button-ups. I purposely knock over some chairs that are stored upside-down on the tables. It gets a bit of the frustration out. Not much.

What's happening?

"Okay," I finally shout, throwing my hands in the air. "Do any of you know where my friend went?"

Nothing. Everyone stares at the floors.

"Please," I try. "Something took him and he's going to be in terrible pain without me." Nothing again. I shouldn't have expected that to get me any sympathy. I nab the person who is mopping nearest to me, making the floor so wet we'll probably be able to swim on it soon enough, and grab his face.

"Look at me!" I shout, but it doesn't matter how roughly I clutch him. He doesn't look up from the floor and his reflection in it.

A high-pitched voice calmly says, "Let go of him."

I turn to see a heavyset man with unnaturally black hair standing behind the counter of a fried chicken shop. He walks around to approach me, and I note how impressively short he is, considering we're the same height and I'm never taller than anyone.

"Who gave you the right to come here and manhandle my humans?"

"Uhh—"

"Speak up!" he barks, like a scolding teacher. I look down, not enjoying being at eye level with him, and notice his name tag.

Otis
Manager

"Otis," I say, trying to turn the anxiety off and the charm on. "Fine establishment you're running here. Very, uh, clean. Now we were making quite the spectacle before, so I'm sure you heard, but my friend was in here and then vanished after some sort of shadowy thing grabbed him. Do you have any idea where they went?"

He snorts. "Yeah, I do."

I wait. He stares, his lips pulling up into a smarmy grin.

"Can you tell me?" I ask.

"I can, but I won't."

"Please," I plead halfheartedly, not able to hold my hands together on account of the bandages.

"You do ask rather prettily, don't you?"

His tone sends an uncomfortable shiver up my spine. He looks like the character I immediately distrust in any movie, the bright colors and fluorescent lights making his unwashed appearance more apparent.

"How about this," he says. "I'll tell you what you want to know, but you have to do something for me."

"What? I'll do anything."

It's what people say in films, but I doubt I actually mean it.

"There's a demon named Hagenti who stole my faith. I'd like for you to get it back for me. Bring me my faith and I'll tell you where Ashmodai is."

"Your faith?" I ask. "Isn't that something you have to find inside yourself?"

"No. If my faith was inside of me I would have you look in there, wouldn't I?"

"Right. Of course. Definitely. And it's with—"

"Hagenti."

"Hagenti. Cool." I look down at my feet and take a few deep breaths. There is so much happening, so much to be done, and all of it happening far too fast. I need a break. "Which direction does Hagenti live?"

Otis smiles at me, his grin growing bigger and bigger until it stretches up past his nose and begins slicing a disgusting grimace towards his hairline. I decide to cut my losses and get out of there—maybe the sentient laptop can help—but before I can, he grabs me by the shoulders and leans in. Those aren't lips, they're a disgusting wound, but they press against mine before I can fight back. I freeze. Then I prepare to kick him in the balls except suddenly, I know exactly where Hagenti is. Like someone dropped a bomb in my brain, the information bursts across all my synapses.

Hagenti is in a shop called "Slipshod" in a region called "Endemia" and I know exactly how to get there.

By the time I regain my bearings, Otis is gone.

I jog back to the car, my entire brain a whirl of *Ash is gone. Ash is in pain. It's all my fault because of this stupid bond. That was my first kiss. My first kiss.*

"Marcus, what do I do?" I ask the air, kicking one of my front tires.

I'm talking to no one. No one is going to answer or tell me

what to do. I really hate making decisions sometimes. I move on to kick the other front tire and realize something: I can unbind Ash now. Then, wherever he's gone, he won't be in complete agony.

The sigil for unbinding is simple. I committed it to memory before all this began. It looks like two crow's feet facing away from one another with an *S* between them. Easy. But where to put it? My left arm is out, and I need to use my right one to actually carve the damn thing. My left thigh has the binding mark and I don't want to accidentally turn that into something even nastier. Right thigh it is, then. It won't be the worst thing that's happened to me recently, and I don't hesitate before digging into my back pocket for the grimy knife and getting to work. This time, I don't flinch. I don't cry, or yell, or grimace. Anything can become normal if you let it. I was kissed for the first time. His breath smelled of artificial oranges and I suspect I'll never eat a Creamsicle again.

There is red.

I think about the first time I wore makeup. My leg stings.

Laura spread bright green cream eyeshadow everywhere. It was hideous. The dripping down my leg tickles.

Laura likes to take long showers but I hate it. I wish I could simply put on eyeshadow in the mornings, cover myself in perfume, and call it a day.

It's finished.

I don't feel any different apart from the new stinging gashes on my leg. To match the pain I'm feeling everywhere else, I suppose. Now I only have to be anxious about Ash having potentially been kidnapped. (Demon-napped? That's what I did to him back in Asbury Park to begin with.)

Also, the possibility of having to find Marcus by myself if I don't get Ash back. No. I won't think that.

Also, faith. Faith and a demon named Hagenti. Laura wouldn't believe what I've gotten myself into. Alone in Hell, no guide to be found, and limited amounts of common sense. I rub my bandaged arm on the fresh cuts to try and soak up some of the blood, staining it a brilliant red. I must truly be a sight now, either a completely badass bald apocalypse babe or a total teenage nightmare. Probably the latter. The air is thick and disgusting, which weirdly suits this parking lot where everything feels and looks so filthy. I want to take a shower.

Okay. I take a deep breath and get into the car. *To Endemia.*

The podcast begins playing when I turn on the car. This world may have taken Ash, but at least it lets me have Elle.

CHAPTER SEVEN

**In which there are
dragons and homonyms.**

Hello, my crazy crew of people with too much free time and not enough taste! As you all know, I'm not one for so-called "natural beauty." It isn't my scene. Being a wonderful and loving person, though, I eventually relented and took Anita to the Grand Canyon like she wanted. She loves all that nature and greenery drivel, and I love her, so . . . there you go. We have this little game where we both pretend to not want to do what the other one does, and in return for me going to the Grand Canyon, I was able to drag her to a piece of Americana I had wanted to see my entire life. She complained the whole way there, and it was wonderful.

My father once told me that the only reason roadside attractions popped up to begin with is because there's nothing else in these areas that could possibly make people want to go. He thought visiting them was a stupid idea because of how their entire existence depends on mundanity. Well look at me now, Daddy!

The road leading to Cadillac Ranch was lined with corn, a blur of green and tan out the window. Definitely a Kansas-from-the-Wizard-of-Oz sort of area, but we got over the rainbow soon enough. Neon flashed past outside, splattered on dumpsters overflowing with cans of spray paint. Thankfully, we had a few cans of our own because I always come prepared to deface property.

The Cadillacs stood like a row of priests in the distance and we ran to them, sinking into mud with every step. It was one of the first times I didn't care about the state of my shoes. The cars were surrounded by shallow pools of water from a recent rainstorm and I tried to balance precariously on whatever bits of dry land were left. I painted a pink heart on the side of one car, drew two vowels inside and a plus in between them. I painted the words *save bees* on the next car over. Anita painted the words *not my president* on the ground in a spot that would have been impossible to miss while approaching the area.

A couple appeared. The woman

had the hair of a news anchor and was holding her iPhone raised high in the air, obviously livestreaming to social media. She shouted, "Look at these two girls!" in a voice as sharp and sugary as rock candy. I lowered my head and ran.

I wish I could do that. Lower my head and run. Instead, I drive straight into my problems and am always so surprised when that course of action turns out to be problematic. The world beyond my windshield is mostly normal, but perverted enough that I can't get comfortable. It feels like I'm driving down ordinary suburban roads when suddenly, a deer with eight legs and flaming antlers starts galloping alongside the car. Then, I pass something that looks like a public swimming pool with clowns instead of lifeguards. It's hard not to rubberneck with shit like that going on outside.

Endemia, the region of Hell I'm headed towards, is the strange mix of unexpectedly close and too far that everything seems to be down here. It feels lonely in the car and I consider cracking open the supposedly sentient laptop for company, but I'm not that desperate yet. The weirdly suburban roads gradually turn more urban. Or, at least, what I imagine people who have never visited Manhattan think "urban" is. As the buildings become taller and more rustic, the streets become emptier, only the occasional car driving by at a pace so slow it couldn't be imitated, and it gives me *déjà vu*.

Knoxville, Tennessee.

Not that I've ever been there, of course, but Elle has, and this main street looks exactly the way I always pictured it in my head, which is ridiculous since I'm certain I was never picturing it accurately. There aren't any photos on her website. But, just as she describes it in *Rich Bitch*, there's a sign for Gay Street hanging from a traffic light and a beaten-down cinema with the word TENNESSEE written down the side with lightbulbs. It's as if someone plucked the picture right out of my mind.

The Knoxville portion of her podcast is a great sequence. She calls it a "city of firsts" because it's where she tried her first phosphate—a predecessor to the ice cream soda—and first plate of grits. She complains about how the "drugstore" is actually an ice cream parlor and flashes back to time spent in Montmartre getting up to some risky business. All wonderful things to aspire to and dream about. All of it right here. I avoid looking at the building labeled "drugstore" as I drive past, the temptation already being too great. I try not to focus on anything for long, worried that if I do, I'll start to notice whatever makes this place Hellish. Headless horsemen or cannibalistic ostriches or something.

Slipshod is beyond the city proper, on the other end of the oh-so-tempting main street. From the outside, it looks like a looming cement warehouse, a bit beaten down, except it has the name hanging above its door in rainbow letters. All caps. I park and don't think twice before getting out of the car and walking inside.

The first thing I see is a tube television that has been turned into a fish tank. Cool. Then I look beyond that and realize I have entered a labyrinth of weird crap.

Dresses too long to fit any woman hang on a wall, and beads shaped like hot dogs are strung along the power cables winding along the floor. There are pistachio instant pudding boxes stacked into the shape of a spade. I go to inspect them more closely when a voice comes from my left.

"Who are you?"

A girl, probably around my age, with a long gash through her left eye, is speaking. The brutal scar stretches up past her hairline, leaving a bald patch in her red hair. She must be Hagenti. Not as terrifying as I'd anticipated. In fact, she's actually quite beautiful, but so far nothing down here has turned out the way I anticipated. It seems like shape-shifting is as much of an everyday occurrence as brushing your teeth, but maybe that metaphor is irrelevant considering no one here seems to brush their teeth. Who would have expected some demons in Hell to look like young models? Maybe this is a honeypot.

"Nice to meet you. My name is Jules. I'm here on behalf of a demon named Otis. He wants his faith back."

Her eyes darken and whatever hint of a smile that had been resting on her lips falls away completely. What a shame. It was a lovely smile.

"Are you?" she says, sounding unimpressed and slightly malicious. "Well, don't let me stop you. Go and have a look for it."

The expression on her face is one of subdued recognition. She obviously knows what this faith looks like, but I decide not to push my luck and ask for any hints. Something about her bearing makes me think it's better not to bother her any further. Hopefully I'll know it when I see it. I give her a small nod and walk past the counter into the mess of the shop interior, my hand remaining wrapped around the knife in my pocket the whole time.

I pass through pile after pile of glorious garbage. Coloring books, dolls, and cassette tapes. This place has the appearance of a maze but with only one pathway to walk through. Records, CDs, and used postcards. An old photograph of a woman I will never meet. Stacks of magazines stretch up to the ceiling, towering over bins of broken Furbies, ukuleles, and death metal posters. In a different setting, this would be a landfill, but add some walls and shelves and suddenly it's a shop. *A hoard.*

The place is split up into little cubby-like areas that shoot off from the main path. There is some sort of organization at play but I can't seem to crack what the rules are. I walk into one of these areas slowly, picking up every trinket inside that catches my eye and then placing them back exactly where I found them. Clothing and flowers made of dusty fabric. Calendars from years long gone or not yet come to pass. Nothing that I would identify as faith. I have half a mind to go back and double-check some crates of records for a copy of *Faith* by George Michael.

I move onto the next section of the shop and have the realization that, given my short stature, there's a lot above my head that I haven't been noticing. This place has ceilings as high as a warehouse, and objects dangling from the beams by chains. Not to mention what's perched on top of the shelves.

Look up, I tell myself, chanting it like a mantra in my head. *Look up.*

After searching and searching for who knows how long, I decide it's time to get intimate with those higher-up objects. There's a sturdy-enough-looking bookcase nearby that has shelves filled with bright yellow hardcover editions of Nancy Drew. I knock off all the books on one side of it and climb up. From there, I jump to another shelf that lines up with the top of the "walls," there being nothing but an empty void between those and the stupidly high ceilings. A few plastic alarm clocks fall to the floor, cracking when they collide with poorly carpeted cement, but I get up there with only one arm to help me. *Suck it, Spider-Man.*

Perched up above the ground like this, I can see the entire layout of the shop, and my chest goes all sorts of funny at the realization that it might be never-ending. Sure, there's a wall behind me, but I can see over all the aisles and the cubbies pretending to be rooms, and there's no sign of an end. The place stretches out so far there's a horizon line shining the bright white of fluorescents. This might take a while. *Oh, Ash.* He could be anywhere, having anything done to him.

And I was actually starting to like the guy, too.

What would Marcus do?

Actually, no, scratch that. He's a filthy rich British actor. He would pay someone to do this for him. But on the other hand, Fletcher Fatale would already have Otis' faith and be on his way to rescue Ash and sneer lovingly at Ferdinand Ferdinand. So, what would Fletcher Fatale do?

I scan the area again, trying to come up with an effective game plan to get through everything, when my eye catches on an irregularity. Not that the entire place isn't highly irregular, but around three or four sections down and just as many across from where I'm perched, there's a stack of carpets—the fancy sort with tassels on the ends—that is pulsating. They move up and down like a heartbeat, and something about it, some sort of energy, feels distinctly alive. I make up my mind to go investigate.

Climbing down is significantly more difficult than going up, and I end up using my left hand to do it, without bending my arm at all. Not that it matters because, when I'm about three shelves up, the entire thing tilts forwards, and I end up plummeting to the floor, books piling on top of me and the bookcase on top of them, thoroughly reaffirming my foregone conclusion that this is the worst day ever. If this even is a day. I climb out from underneath the pile of musty books and structurally unsound bookshelf parts with a small "ow" merely for the purposes of my own self-pity, and shake it off when I'm on my feet again.

If this was an actual shop, I would panic and do something to clean up the mess I made. Instead, I leave everything on the floor and keep moving.

I don't merely keep my hand on the switchblade, but pull it out of my pocket completely, holding it out in front of me with my good arm as I walk. I feel like Marcus when he played that explorer in a film *The New York Times* called "the most blatant and ineffective rip-off of *Indiana Jones* to ever be produced."

I mailed moldy tomatoes to their office.

The pile of carpets I saw from afar is staggeringly tall. They're all sorts of colors and styles, some resembling the magic one from *Aladdin* and others appearing to have more homey designs, like brown horses mid-gallop. They gently move up and down, a couple feet in either direction, and I try not to think about what it looks like. What it obviously is. I grab the corner of one and pull, knowing—because I've watched enough movies—that some horrible creature's eye will be underneath. Something that will now try to kill me for awakening it from its slumber.

Guess what? I'm completely right.

It's a horrible eye, completely purple apart from the black hole of a pupil looking directly at me. I step backward, wanting to get as far away as possible from a creature whose eyelashes alone are the same size as me, and, to my horror, it starts moving.

Rugs slip off and fall to the ground as whatever the hell this is stands. I back up farther and farther, but can't get away. A scaly foot hits the floor in front of me, shaking the walls of the building. Another foot lands next to the first one, taking out a table covered in fine china. The rugs continue to scatter, landing on top of all sorts of junk—myself included—as this horrible body stretches up to the faraway ceilings. *How was all that body hiding under there?* I pause in my slow-motion backing up to deal with the fact that *of course* I would have to face an actual dragon. Typical. I was really hoping I would only have to defeat the pretty girl up front or, at least, convince her to help me. Instead, I face silver scales that reflect the colorful shop and the lights above, pointed claws that are so long they almost reach the floor even while he stands on his hind legs; this monster is something I would love to see in a film.

My switchblade seems humorously pathetic now. I stick it back into my pocket in defeat.

"Who are you?" the dragon asks, his voice like a deafening gong, eyes laser focused on me.

The dragon talks. Of course the dragon talks. I'm never going to complain about how boring New Jersey is after this.

"Uh . . ." I say. "Uh . . ."

"Her name is Jules," comes a voice from around the corner. The girl from up front. *Oh no.*

"Jules," growls the dragon. His voice sounds disused, like he has been chain smoking for far longer than I've been alive. That's a mental image I would enjoy in most other circumstances. "Sounds unimportant."

"I think she's that girl The Fates are after. Don't know where the demon is. She came in alone." The girl delivers all this like she has solved some marvelous puzzle, but the inside of my brain is nothing but question marks.

"The Fates are after me?" I ask. "What?"

"The job's already been done, though, so she's a bit useless to us now."

"Obviously," the dragon responds, both of them pointedly

ignoring me. I turn to try and leave, but the girl blocks my path. "Doesn't mean we can't have some fun with her, though."

The dragon lifts a glistening foot, and I run at the girl, throwing all my weight into pushing her out of the way. Evidently, all my weight isn't that impressive because within seconds, she has me on my back as she straddles my thighs, an immovable force. The dragon hobbles over and stands on top of her, making us this weird sandwich of poor choices.

"Let her go, Faith," he says, and I stop thrashing about to look her dead in the eye.

"You're Otis's faith?" I ask, not believing my bad luck.

"No. If I'm anyone's, I am Hagenti's, but I like to think I am my own."

Then I make a wild guess based on how my life seems to be working out. "Hagenti is the dragon, isn't he?"

"Bingo," she says as she stands up and crosses her arms, looking down at me. "Now run." I don't need to be told twice. Scrambling to my feet, I back up while brandishing the switchblade as if it could protect me from either of my foes, then break into a sprint. Hagenti only takes two steps that shake the shop and knock me into the shelves before he's already in front of me again. The aisles are small, though, and he can't turn around, so I run through them and veer to the left, nearing the front entrance.

Then I'm flying.

Surely *that's* something I would remember knowing how to do.

My ass promptly hitting the ground again is a stark reminder that defying gravity is not actually a skill I possess. Hagenti had picked that moment to drop down on all fours and shake the shop, myself included, with him.

"Do you like games?" he asks. The question feels like a trap, so I don't answer. "My pet is also a little girl, and she loves games."

"She *likes* games," Faith mutters, emphasizing *likes* over *loves*, but the dragon doesn't seem to hear. There's something tricky about her, like I could easily see the dragon being her pet but not the other way around. The front door is ahead—it's actually in my line of sight. I'm sure there's a world in which I run straight out, jump in the car, don't look back, and potentially end up incinerated, but Marcus needs me. I keep telling myself that. *Marcus needs me.*

For some reason, though, the only man I picture in my head is Ash. Ash, being stolen by shadows. Writhing in pain. His screams. Ash as an angel. Ash in a margarita button-up shirt.

In terms of other worlds, there's probably one where we could be friends. Drinking buddies. Co-workers.

Ash needs me.

With the dragon down on all fours, he seems to be about ten or fifteen feet tall. He gives chase as I run past the entrance and into the rest of the shop. You know, like an idiot. How am I already being chased by another mythical creature? Hasn't that happened enough since we came here? Valac and The Fates. I wish I had a pair of scissors strong enough to stab this guy in the neck.

I glance up at him to reassure myself that his neck is made of silver and not anything I could have a go at with a modicum of success. It's for the best that this is all happening to me and not someone with any real self-preservation instincts. If this were Laura, she would still be in the planning phase. Actually, if this were Laura, she would have been smart enough to not have even gotten tied up in all this.

Then it dawns on me. The eyes. They're not silver, they're all fleshy and weak and *there*. I look at my switchblade and know I'm not willing to lose it in this fight when there is so much unknown to come.

I run farther and Hagenti overtakes me with a single step. Faith is nowhere to be seen, but I put that thought aside and duck into a section dripping with linen. Sheets of the stuff hang on the flimsy walls and are draped over tables.

I spot a snow globe on one of these tables, and dart over to grab it, not even bothering to shake it up or see what's inside even though that goes against all my basic instincts, and hold it behind my back. Like that's not suspicious.

"I'm ready to play a game now," I shout. Hagenti turns his head from side to side, then spots me as I stand on the table.

"Good," he says, and I think what he's intending to do with his face is smile, but it's difficult to tell with all the fangs involved. As the modern kids say, *yikes*. He doesn't have to lower his head much to be level with me where I stand on the table, and the second he's close enough for me to smell his stale breath, I take the snow globe by the base and smash it as hard as I can into his right eye.

He snorts and the strength of it knocks me off the table. I go flying back and, after taking a moment to reorient myself and stand upright, I start running deeper into the building, hoping to put more distance between us while he's discombobulated. That has got to sting.

Ropes, I think. *Or chandeliers. A net. Anything!*

I can't kill him, that's obvious enough, but trapping him, half blind, for long enough to grab Faith and run is the only idea I can think of. I guess that's the one I'm going with.

There is a rainbow-colored parachute ahead, hanging off the corner of a wall. *Perfect.* I can trap him in it, challenge him to a battle of wits for Faith, win, whisk her away, and save everyone. Except my brain catches up with me and I realize there's nothing in this shop strong enough to capture a dragon made of silver. Nothing that I can think of while stressed out like this, and Hagenti isn't the only one I'm going to have to capture.

I leap from an ornate gold chair and grab the parachute, dragging it down. I tear off its long ropes and tie them from one table to the next in between cubbies, then run until the aisle turns. Slowly, Hagenti emerges from where I left him and begins hobbling in my general direction, unsteady on his feet and obviously misjudging the room with only one eye. Even dragons bleed red, and the silver scales on his face are painted the deep crimson of bad mistakes.

I fold the parachute, then tie it around my neck like a cape before knocking a heavy colander off of a shelf to attract his attention.

He runs sloppy and slow, smashing shelves and taking down walls, his head turned to the side to see me with his only working eye.

I feel nothing. Absolutely nothing. It's as if his bellows don't even reach my ears.

He trips over the rope and comes crashing down, causing everything in the vicinity to tumble to the ground. I take off again the second his belly hits the floor, stepping on his front leg as I climb over, and manage to squeeze around his hindquarters. This won't give me much time.

"Faith!" I shout, not knowing where she's gone. "Faith, please, I have to talk to you. I can get you out of here. You don't have to be a pet."

Faith appears, seemingly out of thin air although I suppose she must have come around the corner. She slams into my side, knocking me down yet again.

"Yeah, so I can go back to being Otis's? Not likely."

I don't have a good comeback for that because she's not technically wrong, so I panic and go to my trusty fallback.

Meaning, I shove the knife into her foot.

"Bitch!" she shrieks, bending in half.

"Look who's talking," I shout back, accepting the fact that my sense of empathy truly has shriveled up and died, and I wrap her in the parachute. She flails her arms and the foot with a knife sticking out of it, but I manage to get her all rolled up. Before covering her feet, I yank out the knife and cover the bleeding quickly with fabric. It soaks through instantly. I tie the corners and bunch up the edges, then tuck bits of fabric into other bits of fabric until she looks like a mummy in a pride parade. Hagenti's heavy breathing makes me grateful that Faith is already dead and can't suffocate. Muffled shouts. I ignore them. The dragon bellows. I ignore that, too. It's easier than one might think.

In my head, I'm going to throw her over my shoulder and carry her out of the building, but with one wonky arm and no physical strength whatsoever, that idea dies quickly. I grab a handful of fabric and drag. It's slow going, and her struggling definitely isn't making it any easier, but we aren't terribly far from the front door and I manage to get us both out before Hagenti is on his feet again. He's definitely too big to get out the doors, but the sooner we're gone, the better. I open the passenger door and manage to whack a lot of things that shouldn't be whacked while getting her into the seat. Finally, I buckle the seat belt.

Getting myself in the car and both of us moving is easy. I veer out of the parking lot and drive until we are in, and then out of, fake Knoxville. The city seems to have gotten fuzzier while I was fighting (or, you know, cleverly avoiding) the dragon, with the edges of buildings going slightly blurry and rooftops starting to crumble into the sky. All that matters is that the roads remain intact, and they do. Once we're suitably outside of city limits, I pull over in an area that looks normal enough.

"I'm going to uncover your face now," I say, turning to where she is sitting next to me. I feel moderately cruel, and hope this will stop the shouting. "Don't be scared. I'm going to have to use a knife."

Understandably, she screams that much louder, but the parachute slices easily and soon her face is freed. And extremely angry.

"You're a monster," she seethes with absolute certainty.

"No, your old owner was a monster, and I saved you from him. You're welcome."

She spits at me. I probably deserve it—if not for this then for something else.

"You don't know anything. You're the monster and Otis is worse than all of you. I hate you!"

Realizing that this is a battle I'll never win, I turn straight ahead and keep on driving. I don't doubt Faith; from what I've seen, it isn't difficult to believe that Otis is horrible. But Ash is in trouble, and it's not like she wasn't just literally the possession of an actual fucking dragon.

There are people out the window holding blank street signs high above their heads.

Behind them, the trees writhe like they're in agony.

107

I hate silence. I hate driving in it most of all. I would turn on the podcast but even I'm not that cruel; I'm a fangirl but also somewhat self-aware. Faith is having a bad enough day as it is.

"Can I ask you one thing?" I say.

"No."

She really means that *no*, judging by her tone.

"How did you manage to go rogue like this? To escape your punishment and end up in the clutches of a dragon? Did he kidnap you like in a fairy tale?"

"If anyone's kidnapped me, it's you."

"Yeah but—"

"Are you really asking me how I've gone rogue when it's obvious you've done exactly the same thing?"

Once again, she's not wrong. Her voice is nice to listen to. A bit nasally. It's cute. I decide to risk hearing it again.

"Was being the cashier for a dragon really so much better than that whole eternal janitor business Otis has going?"

I'm happy her hands are trapped, otherwise I'm certain that question would've gotten me smacked.

"Of course it was. Are you stupid? Hagenti is my friend and he keeps a magnificent hoard. You, on the other hand, are a traitorous bitch who I can only hope finds herself getting stepped on by a dragon in the not so distant future."

I could listen to her insult me all day. Part of me wants to keep "poking the bear" so to speak. Instead, we drive in silence, and I pretend that doesn't make my insides crawl. Giving in, I turn on the podcast with a silent apology to my passenger.

Hey there! I want to start off today's episode by answering some questions that have been getting sent in to the website. The first one is jumping the gun a bit in terms of where we are in the story, but too many of you asked for me to ignore it. There were multiple comments wondering about my favorite

place I've visited in America and my
answer is, hands down, the Kaskaskia
Dragon. Now this is skipping ahead a
bit in the narrative I've been attempting
to construct, but there is this absolutely
fantastic metal dragon who wears an
Abraham Lincoln top hat in Illinois. If
you buy a special coin from the liquor
store across the street from him, you
can stick it into a box in the dragon's
foot and he breathes actual fire.
There are propane tanks—

"Did you headbutt my CD player?" I ask, trying to hide that
I'm impressed.

"How else was I supposed to make that garbage stop?"

"Fine. What do you want to listen to, then?"

"Nothing. Let's listen to nothing."

The trees outside continue to writhe.

"Why don't you tell me about your life on Earth?" I say,
having no idea why I'm trying so hard. I'm pretty decent at
telling when I'm not wanted, which is typically whenever I'm
around people and Fletcher Fatale is mentioned. Being around
Ash recently has allowed me to practice ignoring those signals,
though.

Faith doesn't speak. I finally decide to take the hint and drive
in silence, as horrible as it sounds. She's not much older than me,
and she looks like the sort of person I can imagine befriending
in college. Spunky. Pretty. Willing to argue with me.

What a shame.

The sky looks ready to swallow us up and it must take five
times as long to drive back as it did to drive out to the shop, every
second crawling across my skin like an army of ants. Whenever
Faith shifts, the parachute produces a long polyester scream that
grabs my attention.

We drive and drive and I think about Ash. About who that

shadowy figure might be, and if the unbinding even worked, and why they want him.

Why are The Fates after us? I know we were slightly indecorous, but it's over now. I have a feeling we triggered something much greater than we intended.

I actively choose not to consider whether or not Ash is in trouble because of me.

I pull up to the rest stop and park directly in front of the doors, not bothering with the parking spaces. Faith is heavy and I can only do so much.

Car in park. Out the door. Open hers up. There are tears in her eyes. Not a lot, and none that have fallen, but they're red and watery and I don't think about what Otis must have done to her. What he's going to do now.

Otis will always be my first kiss.

He doesn't come out to help me carry Faith; I don't know if he even can. I hold her in my arms bridal-style and move impossibly slow, my bad arm burning with every step. It reminds me of carrying bags of groceries in my arms for long distances, refusing to take a car to the shops or to make multiple trips. Alternatively, it reminds me of walking to the gallows, except so much worse. Faith glares at me the entire time, and it's difficult to keep my eyes up and pretend I don't see.

The second we're inside, I lay her down on the floor. Actually, to be brutally honest, it's more me dropping her on the floor than me laying her gently down, but she doesn't seem to hit her head or anything. Otis emerges from the throng of blue outfits and sullen faces.

"You did it. You brought back my Faith." He has the nerve to look surprised.

"I am not yours," she hisses, her first words in a while. I mutter an apology, speaking only to myself.

I'm sorry. I'm sorry. I'm sorry.

Otis smiles down at her, then returns his attention to me.

"Impressive. Well, a deal is a deal. Ashmodai was taken by Gerald Empusa to his Endless War."

"Where's that?" I ask, stone-faced.

"Here, let me show you." He leans in, but this time I'm quicker. I hold my arms up in front of my face and block him.

"No. Not that again. You can tell me. With words."

"Fine, but you're only making things more difficult for yourself." He shrugs. "Do you know of the Well to Hell?"

"The real one or the one down here?"

"Good. Very good. The one down here. He is underneath."

"What?"

"He is underneath. Good luck."

And with that, Otis squats down and picks up Faith, then throws her over his shoulder, much in the way I had hoped to before, and begins walking away. An indescribable feeling comes over me, bubbling up in my stomach then flying out from between my lips as words before I can stop it.

"Faith," I shout impulsively.

She lifts her head slightly.

"I'll come back for you," I promise, not knowing what pile of clichés I grabbed that one out of and regretting it almost instantly.

I leave before I see where they go.

CHAPTER EIGHT

In which spoons and the
family Surufel are introduced.

Dear Marcus,

I wrote an essay for class today about Hamlet *and* Romeo and Juliet. *I tell you this because I know you've been in productions of both, so I imagine you would be a fan of my essay. Not to mention, your daughter is obsessed with everything by Shakespeare. I think I'll print out a copy and mail it to you with this letter.*

I wanted to title the essay The Salt of Our Youth *but Ms. Hyland said that didn't sound professional enough, which is ridiculous because not only is that title a direct line from Shakespeare, but it's a glorious pun about the fact that I'm writing about young people who are extremely salty. She made me retitle it* The Textualization and Performativity of Youth in Shakespeare's Romeo and Juliet and Hamlet. *Yawn. The topic is interesting, though. I'm showing absolute proof that the three title characters are teenagers. That's obvious for Juliet because her age is in the text, but for the others, I had to do some digging.*

My personal favorite point is about how teenagers don't have an accurate understanding of death, thus making them more reckless, violent, and suicidal. I'm going to stick chemistry and all sorts of brain science into this piece and there won't be a college in America that'll turn me down afterward.

Recklessly yours,
Julia R. Tolliver

I scramble into Absinthe, and without bothering to buckle up, reverse out of the parking lot, driving faster than I've ever gone before. Faster than what should be physically possible. I don't think twice about it. I turn on the radio, ejecting the podcast before it can even begin. Cher is singing.

I sing along, leaning into the steering wheel and whacking it in rhythm. I hit the main road and honk the horn. "I got you babe!"

I stick an arm out the window, and I scream, "Babe!"

If I make it through all of this, I'm writing Cher a thank-you note back on Earth. Or maybe I can convince Ash to give her some special afterlife perks one day.

Who am I kidding? Cher will never die.

A constantly morphing landscape of monsters and images that have been forever burned into my mind flies by in a blur of dismal greys and shocking reds. They make me drive even faster. Sing even louder.

I like this, the singing and driving. For a moment, I almost trick myself into feeling the first dregs of joy. I shove it away.

Marcus. Elle. Laura.

I keep thinking of the people who rely on me, whether they know it or not. *Faith.*

Ash. Ash. Ash.

It keeps me focused as the land flies by. It doesn't allow me to dwell on how weirdly coincidental it feels that the Well to Hell is one of the only landmarks Ash had bothered to point out to me.

How everything still feels like a dream.

I pull up to the Well to Hell. It looks like an old-fashioned sort of drain, except it's massive and completely terrifying. I'm not scared of heights, but no human would be comfortable near a gaping hole this deep; it's in our DNA.

And yet . . .

I get out of the car and run until I've reached the Well, not minding where my feet go. Not minding anything at all.

Take a deep breath. Take a large step.

I jump in. It's that easy. Falling is frightening until it becomes normal. Everything can become normal after a while. Which is exactly how long I fall for: a while. Wind rushes past my cheeks and through the stubble on my head. It's difficult to decide whether I feel more like Alice going down the rabbit hole or a suicide victim who chose an unfortunately tall building.

The pinprick of light that is the sky grows smaller and smaller until it's so dark I can't even see my arms, like I am wading through the black.

Is this what Ash felt like when he was kicked out of Heaven?

No. He said that was sinking, not falling, but I suppose those are two sides of the same coin.

Marcus, I pray, *please make it all okay.*

I hit the ground with a thud and land on dirt. Miles and miles of brown and beige, with barbed wire poking out haphazardly. The sky is a blanket of grey showing no evidence of the hole I just fell from. There's a fire in the distance and piles of clothing everywhere. The air is humid. All of this is easily ignored, though, because for as far as the eye can see, there's nothing but naked people brutally fighting one another with what appear to be extremely long spoons.

You'd think I'd be used to all this otherworldly crap by now, but that seems a bit surreal even compared to everything else I've witnessed so far in Hell. I decide to freak out about it later, though, because analyzing the increasingly avant-garde nature of the world around me definitely won't help get Ash back.

There's a sign directly in front of where I landed, written in a variety of mismatched fonts and wrapped in all sorts of barbed wire and chain link.

Mister Empusa's Endless War!
Please leave all clothing at the door,
then take a long spoon
and join a platoon.
Keep fighting, 'cause we don't keep score.

"Spoons. Spoons," I mutter while getting on my feet. There's a bin of them directly behind the sign.

"Ah ha!" I say, channeling Ash. I grab an ornate one, like the sort a grandma would display with colorful thimbles and cross-stitching, except it's about three feet long.

"Into the fray," I whisper like it's something I thought up myself, but it's actually a line from an animated film. Still, I lean into the badassery, grip the spoon tightly in both hands, and run into battle. Clothed, though. I have my limits, and the nakedness of all the people around me is one of them. My closest point of reference for the dirt in this desert is the New Jersey sand, and I channel all my experiences running from boys and security on the beach into sprinting through the heat. I can feel the dirt getting into my bloodstained socks as I sink into it, the heavy air embracing me as I make my way into battle, crop top and all.

It isn't long before an older, greying woman with sagging breasts begins to spar with me.

I say "spar" like I have the faintest idea what that word means other than the fact Marcus once used it in a film and then began hitting people with swords. Whatever this lady and I are doing, though, neither of us are very good at it, which I guess makes it a fair fight.

"Have you seen a young guy, dark skin, with a shaved head and a ridiculous shirt?" I ask as we clank kitchenware together haphazardly. The woman pulls back in shock before remembering herself and continuing to fight.

"You're the first person I've seen wearing clothes for as long as I can remember."

"Damn."

I spin away from her, undoubtedly feeling much cooler than I look, and find a new partner. An aging bald guy. Chunky. Not unattractive.

"Have you seen a twinky young guy with a shaved head?"

"Not recently, but I sure would like to."

I move on again, asking everyone I can shake a spoon at about where Ash might be. A few people are thrown by the word "twinky," and some even more so by the fact that anyone is bothering to speak to them. The clothes probably don't help, either. No one is trying particularly hard to get any decent hits in, so I'm able to work across the battlefield quickly. I decide to try a different tactic to put things together.

"How did you end up here?" I ask the next woman. She appears to be in her early twenties and looks far too sweet to be fighting in a place like this.

"Mister Empusa. I call him Gerald. Why, is that not how you ended up here?"

"Um . . ." I begin, then dart away to the next person to avoid thinking of an answer. "Who's Gerald?"

"You don't know Gerald?"

"Assume I'm an idiot."

"The hottest man in all of creation? Has a golden leg inlaid with gems? Gerald Empusa? A bit hard to miss considering this is his war."

I move on.

"Do you know where Gerald Empusa is?" I ask, and the person blinks at me before delivering the most violent whack yet, which I take to the stomach and stumble out of the way.

"Gerald Empusa?" I continue to ask. "Have you seen Gerald Empusa?"

My arms grow increasingly tired but my mind stays keen. I carry on like this for what must be hours, but might only be minutes.

Or maybe it's been hundreds of years and my parents are long dead. Friends passed on into oblivion with only their children's children to remember their names.

I care about that deeply, but also not nearly enough. Not right now.

There's one common theme among all the people I speak to: no one seems to hate Gerald Empusa for doing this to them. In fact, they all seem weirdly protective of him. I might even be tempted to say "in love," but that's only because what I see in their eyes is similar to what I feel for Marcus at two in the morning when I'm feeling particularly lonely. The heat isn't making any of this easier, although I'm grateful it isn't as agonizing as the blazing sun in Drizzlyland.

Finally, I stick my spoon into the ground and throw my hands into the air.

"One of you has to have seen the demon Ashmodai or Gerald Empusa, and if you don't tell me where either of them are right now, I'm going to really lose my shit!"

Everyone within a few feet stops fighting to look at me for a moment, but then they all blinkingly return to their task. There's a scene in *Lord of the Rings* where the attractive human with the long hair is frustrated and kicks a helmet while screaming. I look for a suitable projectile to recreate that with, for the sake of my own personal sanity, when a voice stops my hunt.

"I hear you've been asking for me," comes an impossibly deep tenor. Whoever this is could teach motorcycles how to rev. I turn around to see a man with a golden leg, gemstones inlaid. Damn, that girl wasn't kidding. A rainbow of colors, they reflect sunshine that isn't even there. It's blindingly beautiful.

He's naked. I'm used to it by now, having spent a frankly unreasonable amount of time swinging spoons at people in

117

nothing but their birthday suits. His arms are also roughly the size of my head, which I'm less used to. Maybe naked is inaccurate, though, considering he does have on a comically tall black top hat and anachronistically modern sunglasses, in comparison to everything else.

"Gerald Empusa?" I ask, slyly reaching for my spoon.

It's not the best line of defense, but it's something. He must notice because he grabs it himself, then catches his reflection in the silver handle and checks his teeth.

"Yes, that's me. And I don't seem to remember inviting you down here to my little battlefront."

"You didn't. But I have reason to believe that you took my friend and I need him back."

He laughs at that, a deep laugh from his belly, which he holds like some sort of cartoon character. "Oh, you need him? News flash, honey. I need him more. Or, at least, I thought I did. You're kind of ruining it."

"You know who I'm talking about?"

"Yes, but even if I didn't, I think your shouting his name like some sort of auctioneer was enough of a giveaway. I'm going to make this easy on you," he says while removing his glasses with the hand not holding my spoon. "Why don't you come with me?"

He stares into my eyes intently, almost as if he's trying to make something happen. I feel myself cringe as he leans towards me.

He lets out a horrible laugh.

"That's rich," he says, replacing his glasses. "Does Ashmodai know?"

"Know what?"

He doesn't answer right away, instead opting to wave one muscular arm above the dirt next to him like some cheap conjurer. The land rises up to meet his fingertips, then begins shaping itself. Clumps of dirt whirl around as if stuck in a tornado until it forms a mound a bit taller than me.

He lowers his hand and blows on the pile.

Brown eyes. Tan skin. A face I have looked at more often

than my own.

Laura.

He transformed the dirt into Laura. Without thinking, without even breathing I take a step forward, then another, dragging my eyes up and down her form, then freeze.

She's here. The implications sink in. Laura is here. Laura is in Hell and it's all my fault.

No. No. No.

I fall to my knees directly in front of where she stands and look up at her freckled cheeks. Hair in braids.

"Laura?" I whisper. She moves for the first time, reaching a hand down to me ever so slowly. We lock eyes for a moment. Two. Three.

Something is wrong with her face. Holes. There are holes forming on the left side of her face.

"Laura?" I repeat, moving to stand up. To do something to help. Before I can, a strong wind blows past. She crumbles into dirt, her head falling from her shoulders horribly and blowing away in a cloud of brown, and I make no sound. I do not move until she is completely gone and it's just me and the empty air.

I feel feverish. Delusional. Like there's something missing inside of me, inside of my head. Gerald Empusa steps directly into my line of vision.

"What was that?" I grind out from between my teeth, finally getting on my feet again. "Was Laura really here? Please tell me she's alright or ... or ..."

"Don't worry. Your little lady friend wasn't here. That wasn't her. That was a memory."

I look him dead on.

"Why?"

I don't add any other words. No *Why did you do that?* or *Why her?* Simply, "Why?"

"Because I wanted to double-check something. You like girls, don't you? And you don't merely like them. No. You have an enormous capacity to love them. Biblically speaking, that is. And Ashmodai has no idea. Poor bastard."

"What . . . he doesn't . . . I mean . . ."

Like girls. The words echo through my mind, resonating at a fever pitch in my ears, and I'm empty inside. Where my emotions, thoughts, feelings used to be is hollow. Instead, I'm filled with repressed memories of lingering looks at Laura and secret fantasies at night about Elle.

Ones I tried so hard to forget by morning.

And what does Ash have to do with it?

I'm not certain what happens, but the next thing I register doing is punching Gerald's chest repeatedly while chanting, "It's not true!" which probably doesn't help my argument much. But it can't be. I'm not … like that. I'm not. I love dresses and makeup and watching romcoms. I love Marcus K. Dixon and I love the fact that Fletcher Fatale secretly loves another man, even if people think I'm making it up. I love him, and he is a man, and I like men. Only men. These are things you know by the time you're seventeen. I've never met a lesbian that I've related to.

I've never met a lesbian.

Is *lesbian* even the right word?

He holds me back by my shoulders so my little flailing fists can't reach him. "Disagree with me if you want," he says, "but I am never wrong. It isn't possible."

I'm having a sexuality crisis forced on me in the middle of some War of the Spoons by a cyborg-looking man. This must be another trick. Hell does that, Ash told me. This man is trying to freak me out.

"I'm going to bring you to Ashmodai. This is too good."

As what I assume is a peace offering, Gerald holds out my spoon and I take it by the handle, sniffling and feeling pathetic.

"I'd be more upset about how I wasted time on the two of you, considering your apparent uselessness, but honestly, I've never liked The Fates much and this is their fight."

This was also because of The Fates? How many demons have they sent to destroy us?

This one certainly isn't trustworthy enough to ask.

He leads me away, walking in a serpentine pattern through the throngs of sinners. They all stare when he passes, and look as if they want nothing more than to go to him.

"Have you enjoyed your time in my humble little patch of Hell?" he asks smoothly, almost like we're friends.

"It certainly is creative," I say, which is a lot more coherent than my internal monologue of screaming.

"Thanks. When I inherited it, they told me I could do with the land as I please. This is what I please. It thrills me to see, and I get to see it forever."

I don't say anything to spur him on, still assuming that all of this is a trick, but Gerald keeps on talking.

"You know, when The Fates described you, I expected much less, but you did an admirable job of fighting out there. Wielded the spoon bravely. Not as good as—"

"Wait," I interrupt, not able to keep quiet about it anymore since we're apparently chatting now. "The Fates described me to you too? Why? What kind of game are they playing?"

He side-eyes me, as if he realizes he's said too much, but then decides he doesn't care. "They want you . . . out of commission. Surely you know this considering they've already succeeded. I heard a rumor that they sent Stymphalian birds after you guys. I wish I'd known of your condition before, though. I'm not in the business of hanging around rest stops on the upside to pick up my lovers, and obviously I'm not going to get the reward for Ashmodai that I expected."

Reward? Condition? "Lovers?" That last question is the only one I actually manage to vocalize.

"It's what I call the people who spend their time here with me. They love me and I love them."

The heat is brutal on my closely shorn head, and the sand gets everywhere. It itches. At least it's much easier to navigate with everyone parting for us like the Red Sea in films. No one gets in Gerald's way, so no one gets in mine.

"And they love that you love them?" I ask, eyeing a particularly decrepit-looking old man.

"Certainly. It isn't always obvious but I can tell. I have a sixth sense like that."

He seems to be able to do a lot with that sixth sense, from determining people's sexuality to making them fall in love. Maybe I should invest in one of those, not that I'll need it. Marcus will have little choice but to fall for me once I bring him back from not only the dead, but also eternal torment.

We'll have to wait a year or two to date—until it's legal and less creepy—but I'm patient.

We walk to the outer fringes of the fighting and I spot Ash in the distance. Before Gerald can try to stop me, I run to him. Ash is currently engaged in some pretty intense-looking roughhousing with another guy of a similar build and bearing. I immediately shove this stranger to the ground and face Ash dead on.

"Ashmodai!" I shout. He narrowly stops his spoon from hitting me across the head.

"Jules?" he asks, tenuously. I'm so relieved to see him that his nakedness doesn't even phase me.

"I'm so glad I found you."

I give him a hug, which he doesn't return. That makes sense. This isn't something we've done before, not like this, and I doubt my denim shorts are particularly comfortable pressed up against certain parts of his anatomy.

"What a happy reunion," Gerald says behind me, and immediately Ash wiggles out of my arms and crosses to him like a man in a trance. Actually, no. Not like a man in a trance. Like a man who's been drugged. I've seen this before, when Laura and I snuck into the bar with three cans of Four Loko in her handbag. She kept going to the bathroom to refill her gin and tonic glass with our own alcohol, and once she came back different. This type of different.

But I don't want to think about Laura right now.

"What did you do to Ash?" I ask Gerald, rounding on him.

"The same thing I do to the rest of them. Poor dear, it seems to have affected him pretty harshly. Maybe because he isn't technically dead. Or because of his past as an angel. Or his present as a demon. Could be a whole lot of reasons, really; this is all new for me as well."

Ash leans his head on Gerald's chest and curls into him, which fills me with an unexpected rage. Honestly, though, when was the last time I felt something "expected"?

"Get your hands off him," I say in the closest approximation to a growl my seventeen-year-old vocal cords can manage.

"With pleasure," Gerald responds, and his grin makes me worry I asked for the wrong thing.

"Ashmodai, dear," he says, lifting up Ash's chin with a finger. "You mean nothing to me." He pushes Ash away but doesn't stop there. Gerald grabs my bad arm and plants me in front of my hazy-eyed and sad, stumbling demon.

"You see Julia here? I know you love her. I don't know why, but for some reason you do. Guess what? She doesn't love you back." Ash's face falls even more. "She loves women she's never even met and girls who don't give a rat's ass about her more than she could ever love you. Now kiss."

I am pushed violently into Ash.

It's terrifying. Disgusting. Confusing. It's familiar.

Everything makes sense to Ashmodai Surufel. The fact that there is an Earth beneath his feet makes sense. The other members of the Surufel family tell him so, and People who once lived there pass through his doors on their way to Forever. He has heard such wonderful things about Forever. Beautiful, floating things.

His little hat makes sense. His crimson coat with golden buttons makes sense. Once, one of the People from the world below told him he looked like a bellboy while they were passing through. He asked, "May I take your luggage?" as he usually does, and they laughed. It was a tinkling sound that made his brain fizz and pop happily to hear, but he couldn't understand what was so funny. That's what he always asks People. It's his job, and a job he likes because of the Things in the Luggage. Mainly the clothing. They all make unbelievable amounts of sense and fit into his brain marvelously well.

People tend not to talk much, not to him. They love him, though, and it fills the area behind his gold buttons. The family Surufel loves him, and someone in Forever does, as well, although he can never quite figure out who. That's fine. How wonderful to be loved. How warm.

Ashmodai Surufel never does anything extraordinary. He is never asked to. What he does is his job and that is done well. So well that Someone is impressed.

"Congratulations," Menadel Surufel says. "You are being promoted."

"Promoted," Ashmodai Surufel repeats out loud, tasting the rightness of the word in his mouth and enjoying the way it falls drippingly from his lips. "What does that mean?"

"It means that you are to become a guardian angel. Since this is your first go, we're giving you one human to watch over. Steer her correctly."

"One of the People?"

"Indeed. She will be born tomorrow and you will love her unequivocally, like how we all love you. Watch over her. Guide her. If you do well, we will give you more charges in the future."

"Thank you, sir, but I'm not certain I am qualified. All I know about People is what they bring in their luggage."

"Don't worry about that."

Menadel Surufel pulls him in for a kiss— the way their kind transfers information—and suddenly Ashmodai Surufel's brain is full of

Everything. He always knew there was a land beneath his doors to Forever, but not to such an extent. The world! And what a beautiful world.

The People are not only the few he sees, but billions and billions beyond what can be counted. All different colors and sizes, with all different interests. So many things to be interested in! Ashmodai gasps and backs away.

"See? Now you know the background. Get out there and await the birth of your girl."

"A girl." Ashmodai Surufel smiles. It's one of the few genuinely happy smiles to have ever been in existence, both on Earth and off it. "What's her name?"

He feels especially clever asking that. Look how much he knows about human social customs already. Promotions are fun.

"Julia Rosenthal Tolliver."

And, impossibly, his smile grows even bigger.

Birth is beautiful. Babies are beautiful. Little houses in the suburbs, and loving parents, and ocean breezes are all beautiful. He loves all of it so much and time passes so fast.

Time. That's one thing he does not love. Ashmodai Surufel is not a huge fan of time. At regular intervals, Menadel Surufel checks up on him, and he always reports back with unrelenting optimism.

"It's been a successful year, sir. I stopped Julia Rosenthal Tolliver from walking into a garbage bin the other day, and I prevented a tick from latching onto her leg while she was taking a stroll with her father in the woods."

"Well done."

Ashmodai Surufel watches Julia learn to talk and make friends. He watches her become interested in the insects that crawl on the earth and the birds that fly above, always looking up and never realizing she was looking at her guardian angel. He watches her, and he doesn't always understand. Sometimes she cries and he can't figure out the cause.

One day, he reports to Menadel Surufel and it's different.

"It's been another successful year, sir. I encouraged the waves of the ocean to not carry Julia Rosenthal Tolliver away seven times this summer alone. But I have a request, sir."

"What is that?"

"I would like to be allowed to actually walk the Earth. I understand so much from when you kindly dropped the information into my head before her birth, but that's only information that lives inside of me, not anything real. I want to experience life like People do, so I can better help Julia Rosenthal Tolliver."

Menadel Surufel shows no emotion. He nods.

"Granted. You have one month's Earth duty. You are not allowed to interact with or see your charge while down there. This is purely a recon mission."

"But—"

"In order to prevent you accidentally running into Judith Rosen—"

"Julia Rosenthal Tolliver."

"Yes, in order to prevent any encounters with her, we are dropping you in a different region of Earth. How does the United Kingdom sound?"

"Sounds appropriate, sir."

Except it doesn't. Anything could happen to Julia Rosenthal Tolliver during a month. She's only seven years old. That's barely a life. But Ashmodai Surufel has dug himself into this so he knows better *than to not accept it.*

There's a woman wearing a dress made out of meat. He knows this because it is printed on the front pages of The Guardian, The Sun, *and* The Daily Mail, *which are prominently displayed next to the M&Ms at this little stand on the street.*

Neat.

Ashmodai Surufel wants to say that London is nothing like the Jersey Shore but that would be lying. He sees the same variety of souls in the People here as over there; they just speak differently and have a peculiar taste in condiments.

Julia Rosenthal Tolliver only likes honey mustard and would never go near anything with a name like "brown sauce."

There is so much to do here, but also nothing to do now that his job has been temporarily taken away. He looks at statues and paintings of dead People and tries to remember if any of them have walked through his doors to Forever. He eats food. It's okay. He drinks alcohol. It's slightly better. Once, while drinking alcohol, he is approached by a man with curly hair and leather pants.

"Next round is on me," he says. It's a lie. The next three rounds are on him. And the cab ride to his flat. And breakfast the next morning. The curly-haired man is obviously underwhelmed by Ashmodai Surufel's attempt at copulation but is still a good sport, which is appreciated.

How wonderful, *thinks Ashmodai Surufel as he leaves the next morning,* that love is something two People can make.

It happens again the next night with a female and he thinks he improves slightly. After trying it out twice, he decides to move on to the next new experience and jumps into the River Thames to give swimming a go, only to find himself getting dragged out by some disgruntled police officers. Pity. Ashmodai Surufel has never actually seen a fish in person before and was looking forward to the experience.

He misses Julia Rosenthal Tolliver.

A film called Harry Potter *is coming out soon and everyone is extremely excited to see what will happen in it. He desperately hopes that Julia Rosenthal Tolliver sees it, although he fears she may be a bit young.*

In his final week, he eats beans on toast, jumps over a fence to make it to a Starbucks before closing, attends a protest, attends a counter protest to that protest, and watches a violinist in the tube station for over three hours.

Menadel Surufel meets him in Peckham on his final day, in front of a five-pound cinema that Ashmodai Surufel visited multiple times. It is time to return to his charge.

"It was a successful mission, sir," he tells the other angel. "I have obtained a great deal of practical knowledge that I intend to implement going forward in my role as a guardian of People."

"No, you won't."

"I won't?"

"No," he says, and Ashmodai Surufel realizes that Menadel Surufel is not his usual expressionless self. He seems disappointed. "Copulating with human beings is not permitted. Did you learn nothing from the Nephilim?"

"From the what?"

"It is disgraceful and not behavior we can be seen to endorse. Ashmodai, you are stripped of the Surufel name and hereby sentenced to an endless existence as an agent of chaos in Hell."

And that's it. A scream from lungs that have never screamed before, and the pavement turns squishy under Ashmodai's feet as he is sucked down into an unforgiving void.

Then comes the pain.

He realizes, this is not pain. This is what it feels like to no longer have any Love behind your golden buttons. The screaming goes on.

I pull away from Ash and fall on my ass in an attempt to not back up into Gerald. He approaches me and I crawl backwards, trying desperately to escape.

"No. No."

I'm crying. Are these the same tears I was crying before? Or new ones? How long did that take? I can't look at Ash. My guardian angel.

My guardian angel who abandoned me when I was seven because he had to sleep with some Brits. My guardian angel who is suffering forever because he wanted to do a better job of caring for me. My guardian angel who once loved me more than I can even imagine, but not in that way. Not in the way that Gerald seems to think and I dread. I can't look at him. How can he bear to look at me?

I went from having never been kissed to locking lips far too many times without asking for it.

"What the fuck was that?" I force out.

"I'm assuming that was our darling demon's tragic backstory. What a neat little experiment."

"Experiment?"

I'm furious and scared and still feeling the residuals of Ash's agony from the memory. He groans, and I finally turn my head to look at him. He still seems vaguely roofied, and this is only exacerbated by the fact that when he catches my eye, he promptly twists to the side, braces both hands on the dirt, and vomits. Maybe that will make him feel better.

"Ew," is the only thing Gerald has to say, and I once again

act before thinking and charge at him.

This time, I kick his good leg, the one that isn't golden and liable to break my toes if I hit it the wrong way. I'm not even certain if I'm angry at him or just want to get this confusion out of my system. There's something crawling beneath my skin, like a scream trapped in my throat, and the only way it can come out is by making someone else hurt.

"You bastard!" I shout at Gerald, not certain exactly what I'm referring to in particular, but knowing it's a suitable insult for the situation.

"Little girl, you are becoming more effort than you're worth. Your boyfriend, too."

"He's not my boyfriend," I say through tears, continuing to kick him. "He's my guardian angel!"

"Wow, you two have even more baggage than I thought. No thank you." He holds me back like before. "Look, take him and get out of here. The only stake I had in you two was that favor from The Fates and now there isn't a chance I'll get it. This is far too much drama for me."

I don't have to be told twice. Gerald walks back into his battle and I don't watch him go, instead turning to Ash to see him lying naked in a pool of vomit. An image of him in an apple-red, pristine bellboy suit with a stupid hat flashes before my eyes and I get choked up.

Thank goodness I'm wearing a sports bra, I think as I whip off my yellow crop top and kneel down to clean the sick off of him. I prop him up as he drowsily leans against me, forehead bumping into my chest. I wish I cared more. I try my hand at motherly cooing as I wipe the side of his face with my shirt.

"Sorry," he slurs out.

"For what?"

"For following Mister Empusa. I knew who he was and did it anyway."

"He got into your head. Besides, The Fates sent him after you. They're the ones who've been sending all these horrible things after us. It couldn't be avoided, but I think they've stopped now."

With a strength he didn't possess moments ago, Ash clutches my wrist before I can continue cleaning off his head.

"He's wrong. I don't mind that you like girls and don't like me. I never have," Ash says frantically, like he's trying to justify something. I have never heard him sound so soft. He continues. "There's some love, the protective sort, that lingers inside me. I try to make it go away but it just won't. It's been there since before I fell and I guess he confused it with romantic love. I'm sorry."

The vulnerability is too much for me and I feel like a cruel and unwilling witness to all this nakedness, both physical and emotional.

A beat . . .

"Ash, I do like you," I say, hoping that one word, *like,* expresses the cocktail of emotions currently bubbling up inside me. "And I'm not certain how I feel about girls. Not yet. I . . . I need to think about it. Later."

Ash looks me dead in the eye for a few moments, analyzing, then nods.

"Okay."

He shivers as his body returns to normal. While I hold him in the dirt, a safe distance from any spoons, I wonder if he just experienced the same trip down memory lane that I did. It makes sense that Ash fell for whatever magic Gerald used to bring him here; it's something to do with love and that was violently ripped from him.

He recovers slowly. I don't rush him.

I once had a guardian angel, who was beautiful and full of wonder. And now he looks like someone who had a bit too much fun at a bachelorette party. There's so much we need to figure out. How to get the car back and then how to get to Dolus. And once we get to Dolus, how to get Marcus out of there. How to say goodbye to Ash.

But right now, Ash lies on his back with his eyes closed, looking marginally at peace, and I lean into the fact that it has been an agonizingly long day. Month. Year. Lifetime. I lie next to him and close my eyes, allowing myself to be calmed by the clanging of cutlery in the distance.

CHAPTER NINE

In which some words are said
aloud and many more are not.

Dear Marcus,

Maybe, when I grow up, I'll work with one of your children. They'll take me home to meet you, and you'll instantly fall in love with me. Very scandalous. The tabloids will go insane! It's better that I meet you than they meet my parents, that's for sure. Georgia and James Tolliver are about as boring as two people can get and complete pushovers, too. Sometimes they get all watchful and attentive around me, but they mainly let me do whatever I want.

I can't believe I got stuck with a restaurant manager and a hairdresser as parents when there are people out there who have you as a father. A movie star. I guess marrying one is the next best thing.

All my love,
Julia R. Tolliver

I once read online that lawyers make lists or, at least, the good ones do, so I try to make lists in my head to organize everything that has happened. I add "lesbianism" to one titled *Lenses to Reevaluate My Life Through*, even though I'm not certain that's the right word, and "guardian angels" to one titled *Further Topics I Wish I Learned About Growing Up*.

I'm the first one to try and break the silence. "Ash, I—"

"Don't. Please don't."

I nod. That's fair. A gust of wind comes up and blows the sand so it gets stuck in our bristly hair.

"You aren't bound to me anymore," I say. He remains silent and doesn't look at me, merely gestures to the area of his leg where the mark used to be, now vanished. Sure, there are plenty of other scars scattered over the area, but that specific one is definitely gone. "And The Fates don't seem to be after us now, either. Apparently they didn't waste any time spreading the word that we suck and should be stopped, but for some reason the bad guys don't care anymore."

Ash remains silent. I would have expected three demons setting other demons after us would have gotten more of a reaction, but both times I've brought it up he's remained unfazed.

"You must be uncomfortable, lying in the sand all naked like that. Here, let me ..." I say, trailing off as I stand, looking at anything except for him.

The outer fringes of this land are littered with discarded clothing, and I rifle through a pile until I come up with a soft-enough-looking grey trench coat. Perfect. Ash is now sitting up, so I throw it on his lap and he quickly puts it on to cover himself.

"Thank you."

I wonder if there are superstitions about wearing dead men's clothes. We sit some more. It's nice, just sitting, and for once I don't feel the burning need to face the future. To face my life, and Marcus, the fact that I feel so *wrong*, and that The Fates may or may not want us dead.

There are other things to face, too. Ones even more frightening than all this, which I don't want to think about yet.

Instead, I remember the time Laura helped me do my makeup and she put her hand on the side of my face. I wanted her to never move, even though my eyes were getting tired from looking up as she painstakingly drew on eyeliner.

I'm really not as attentive as I pretend to be, am I? Maybe lawyering isn't for me after all.

Eventually, Ash is the one to take the initiative.

"Come on, then. Let's go. Dolus."

He pats my knee and stands.

"You're still coming along?" I ask. "You heard me. We aren't bound anymore. It's fine."

"In case that wonderful invasion of my privacy didn't clue you in, I have a sort of personal stake in this. I think I'll stick around."

"Thank you, Ashmodai."

"Please, call me Ash."

I smile.

"I guess we carry on now," I say, getting onto my own two feet, the sand sticking to my hands as I push myself up. "But how? We need to get to my car and it's all the way up there." I make a wild sort of gesture with my hands in the general direction of the not-a-sky. "It's at the entrance of the Well to Hell. The one actually in Hell, mind you, not the fake one on Earth."

"Yeah, we're not getting back there."

"We're not?"

"Nope. Once you go down, you don't go back up."

Ash buttons up the coat and ties the sash around his middle as he begins walking, and I hurry after him.

"Fine, then. How do we get to Dolus from here?"

"We walk until we arrive."

"How long will that take?"

"As long as it takes."

Sigh.

"Okay. In what direction then?"

He waves an arm towards where we're already heading, into deeper desert and away from the fighting. "Whichever direction we walk, really."

That doesn't make any sense, I want to scream. *Surely Dolus is back on that layer above us since that's how we were driving to it.*

Except nothing has made sense so, in a way, this actually makes perfect sense.

Everything makes sense, I think, then try to shake that out of my head. Guardian angels and sentient laptops and naked men fighting endless wars all don't make sense. Attraction to females does not make sense. Let me rephrase that: it makes sense for other people, but it has never made sense for me.

Or maybe it does, and that's even more frightening. The silence is thick, laying heavy on my thoughts. I decide to distract myself from one impending crisis by igniting another as we walk toward the horizon, the sounds of war fading to the point of being indecipherable. Anything to get Ash talking again. I have so many questions.

"Why did you appear in my summoning circle instead of Moloch?" I ask.

"Same reason I gave you before."

He obviously doesn't remember the reason.

"That can't be true. That's too much of a coincidence. I think you came because you're my guardian angel—"

"Jules—"

"And you knew I needed help. You came to help me get Marcus back—"

"That's not—"

"Because it's been causing me so much pain and it's your duty to make sure I don't feel any pain."

"I'm obviously not doing a very good job of it!" he explodes, grabbing me by the shoulders for a moment, gripping tight before stepping back with eyes wide and full of something even my future-lawyer brain cannot decipher. "Don't call me your guardian angel. I am not your guardian angel."

"You used to be and there's no reason for us to keep pretending I don't know. How about this: let's play Real or Fake." I don't like the tone I'm using, and even to my own ears

I sound nasty. Mean. I can't seem to stop it. "Did angels start transferring memories by kissing after watching humans make out, or did we pick it up from you guys?"

"I am not answering that. Let's get to Dolus and never speak to one another again. I need some time to lick my wounds."

"If you really wanted us to never speak again, you'd already be gone. Nothing is holding you back anymore. Go if you want."

But I'd rather you didn't.

"You know I'm not going to do that," he says, kicking the sand so it flies into my face. I try to conceal my sputtering. This feels like the desert planet in *Star Wars*, and I wonder if we should be walking in single file to hide our numbers, then force my mind back on track as Ash speaks.

"Fine," he relents. "Let's play Real or Fake."

"You enjoyed sleeping with those humans," I say as we walk slowly, uncertain why that's the first thing I bring up.

"Real."

"You did it out of curiosity and as an expression of love."

"Real."

"You knew it wasn't permitted."

"Fake."

"You love me."

"Real."

"You love me romantically."

"Fake."

"You love me sexually."

"Fake."

I take a breath. "I'm a lesbian."

He gives me a disbelieving look. "It is so not my place to answer that."

Okay. Okay. Fine.

"You're my guardian angel."

"Fake."

Hmm.

"You used to be my guardian angel."

"Real."

"There's some sort of connection between us because of that."

"Real."

"It wasn't severed when you became a demon."

"Real."

"You've been watching over me since I was born."

"Fake."

This stops me short. "You haven't been watching over me since birth? That doesn't make any sense considering I just watched my own birth and, by the way, *ew*."

"I protected you for seven years. You know what happened after that."

"Yes, and I'm deeply sorry, but you must have been watching to have known to come when I was summoning Moloch."

"Actually, no."

I stop, cross my arms, and stare at him, trying to express that there's no way I'll keep walking unless he elaborates. With a sigh, he reaches forward and wipes some blood off of my face that I didn't even realize was there. My body is nothing but blood, scars, and bad choices at this point.

"After I fell, you were my only connection to something I didn't even have a word for. Goodness. The overwhelming feeling of something that is Good. It would be impossible for you to truly understand, but you used to be everything. All of my senses, my occupation, my emotions."

I feel like I just took a sucker punch to the gut. Like the thoughts in my head are taking up too much room and have dissolved into television static. Ash continues to speak.

"I thought that had all been ripped from me and I spent a long time feeling alone and empty, with no way of navigating this new world with these new thoughts. But eventually, I recognized a feeling in myself. It was you. I can't explain it, but you were there and I could sense it. The reason I didn't notice at first was because I was so used to you being everything. Having that morph into a small flicker at the bottom of my stomach was a lot."

He stops walking for a second and closes his eyes. "I knew it was Goodness and I knew it was you. I couldn't watch over you anymore or protect you, but at least I had that. I'm assuming this connection is what made me show up when you tried to summon Moloch. Whatever demonic instincts I had pulled me there, but they were mixed with feelings of you. So I went, and I looked at you, and you looked absolutely nothing like that seven-year-old girl. It nearly broke me right there. I'm not very good at this demon thing but I'm trying my best, and you haven't made it easy on me at all."

The cool breeze carries his words away. The words of a painfully young man wearing only a coat, looking like all he wants to do is run away. I forget my mission and that I'm in Hell. I forget Marcus K. Dixon. I want nothing more than to fall in love with Ash. If this was one of those young adult romance novels I hate so much, it would have already happened, except I can't will myself into doing it. I can imagine a future for myself that has a place for him in it, but not in that way.

The sky is orange. I give him a hug and it feels like an ending.

We walk on, through the infinite landscape. This world feels biblical, like something from a movie where Jesus or Moses will show up and start singing. Which, I suppose, is about right. Maybe when I get back to Earth I'll start going to church or something, considering I now have the inside scoop. Marcus and I will go to church together. Shockingly, that thought doesn't spiral out into some elaborate daydream of our future. *He's why I'm here*, I remind myself. *Marcus did bad things, but he isn't a bad person. I've had weird thoughts but I'm not into girls. We've gotten this far and I think I'm sort of . . . happy.*

"It feels weird to not have you annoying me with that podcast," Ash says, trudging along.

"I can recite it for you if you're that desperate—"

He cuts me off quickly, asking, "How did you find me down here?"

That's one way to change the subject. "It's a long story."

"We have a while."

"Do we?"

"I'm not sure, but there's a good chance we do. When are things ever easy for us?"

Touché. I try to pick a good spot to begin.

"I saw you get snatched up by that shadow, who I guess was Gerald, so I struck a deal with a demon named Otis that resulted in me fighting a dragon in exchange for your location."

"A dragon? Not Hagenti . . ."

"That's the one."

"And you managed to defeat him? That's impressive."

He looks like he doesn't believe me.

"It's really not. I . . ." I take a deep breath. "I had to do something not very nice."

"That happens a lot down here. But if you did it to Hagenti, I'm sure he deserved it."

"No. Not to him. There was a girl named Faith in Slipshod, too. She was so beautiful and she wanted to stay with Hagenti. I kidnapped her and handed her over to Otis."

"Was she originally a resident of Otis' region?" Ash asks, missing the point completely. "Yes, but—"

"Then it sounds like you were doing a service to Hell, getting her back where—"

"*He kissed me!*" I scream, my eyes stinging.

Ash jerks to a stop and looks at me. "What?"

"He kissed me. Just grabbed me and did that. It was my first kiss and it was with a total creep." I take a deep breath and try to calm down. "I understand now that it's some sort of fucked up way of transferring information and he was telling me where Hagenti was, but if he could do something like that, take that from me, who knows what he's doing to Faith right now? She's so beautiful and he wanted her so badly. I promised her I'd come back for her, and I'm worried I lied. And, and . . . and I'm so young."

I'm babbling, but what I'm babbling is the truth.

Ash lets it all sink in. "I'm sorry, Jules."

"It isn't like you haven't kissed me now, too."

139

Because men are allowed to take, take, take, and I am never allowed to *give*.

Ash might as well have been slapped.

"I promise you I had no idea Gerald was going to do that, that he was going to make you kiss me. I wouldn't do that to you. It's not something I even remotely want."

"I know," I sigh, sitting down in the sand for a second while I collect myself. "I'm just angry and you have a face that's easy to be angry at."

He sits down next to me, knees apart and wrists resting on top as we both look towards the horizon.

"Do you think you have feelings for this Faith girl?" he asks.

"What? No. I don't even know her." I don't tack on anything about not being *like that*, and he probably notices. "Even if I did, there's no way she would ever forgive me for this," I add.

"I don't know." He stands. "Forgiveness is easier than you make it sound. I have to believe that everyone in Hell is evil and beyond redemption, otherwise I'd go insane. *You* don't have to be like that, though."

Ash reaches out a hand and pulls me up. There is hope in his eyes. We keep going.

CHAPTER TEN

In which Hell looks
a lot like New York City.

Dear Marcus,

When I'm in college, I'm going to work in a coffee shop. One day you'll be filming nearby and come in to get a drink. I'll pretend not to recognize you, but later that day a production assistant from the set will come by and ask for "the beautiful girl with shining eyes" and I'll know it's me. They'll hand me your number and invite me on set. And that will be the beginning of everything.

Yours,
Julia R. Tolliver

"Dolus!" I shout, grabbing Ash by the arm and pointing to a glimmer in the distance. It might be a mirage, but something about this feels right. "Look, Ash. A city. That's Dolus, right?"

He squints then says, "Yeah. That's it. The epicenter of Hell. Welcome to the city of the damned."

I begin to run ahead but he grabs my arm first.

"Be careful," Ash warns me. "I know you said The Fates seem to have let up, but if they really are sending monsters and demons after us, this will be the perfect place for an attack."

"Got it," I say, falling back in step with Ash even though my body is thrumming with the desire to speed up. The shimmering dot in the distance, wavy in the desert heat, grows larger as we approach. The skyline looks increasingly familiar.

"Is that the Empire State Building?" I ask, once it becomes truly unmistakable.

"Probably. I heard a rumor in Shax's diner that a city on Earth, one that you live near, is based off of this particular section of Hell."

"Not the other way around?" I ask, and he gives me a *seriously?* look that makes me regret ever asking.

Whenever I visit New York City, I take the Lincoln Tunnel from New Jersey. One of my favorite moments is first coming out and feeling like the sun shines brighter than it does in the city, than it had on the other side of the water. Here there are no tunnels. The city just starts. One moment, I'm standing in a strange mixture of dirt and sand that can't seem to decide whether it's a desert or a baseball diamond, the next I'm stepping onto black pavement. Not that there aren't cars here; they all happen to be dangling upside down from traffic lights instead of transporting people.

Ash and I stand next to an empty bodega.

"This is the closest to a capital that exists in Hell," he tells me. "It has many sections and a bad habit of showing up when you least want it to. The closest area is punishment for sinners who liked living in secluded areas. People who can't tolerate the city. Farther downtown is for those who loved nothing more than the sound of their own voice. That's where Marcus ended up, if The Fates weren't lying. In between is a whole mess of rotten things in all sorts of nasty establishments. Tell me, what would you classify as the worst place on Earth?"

"High school."

"Yeah, they have that here."

I shiver.

"We're currently standing in a Manhattan-shaped hotbed of sin and unimaginable suffering."

"Yep."

"Sounds like something Fletcher Fatale would dive headfirst into. Lead the way."

Even in all this insanity, with sparking live wires dangling from signposts and garbage bins that pulsate like they're alive, it's comforting to have Ash next to me. To know that he has some sort of stake in my wellbeing, and I apparently have one in his. Who would've thought?

It only takes a few blocks of treading hard cement to come across something extraordinary enough to make me freeze in place.

"I think I found the hicks," I say, staring dumbly at the sight in front of us. Nothing should have the capacity to shock me anymore. This does. "They appear to be fistfighting human-sized rats."

"Hicks?" Ash asks, keeping his eyes on a person hiding behind a pretzel cart.

"It's a not-very-nice word for people from the country. I'm assuming that's what you meant by those who can't tolerate the city."

A rat with unusually dexterous front paws picks up the cart and throws it.

Ash tells me to keep my head down and follow him, then walks down the sidewalk like he belongs there and has extremely important demonic business to attend to. Mostly naked. With a teenager who looks like she made sweet love to a wolverine.

A man with his hair on fire runs through an upcoming intersection. It becomes increasingly difficult to carry on, but still we walk block after block until I recognize exactly where we are.

"Oh," I exclaim as someone falls from the top of a nearby building and smashes into a bus, setting off its alarms. "We're on 42nd Street. Times Square is that way."

I point in the direction that would be considered "uptown" in most circumstances, and Ash shakes his head. "You really have a death wish if you're thinking about that part of Dolus right now."

"Look, this isn't New York City, it's havoc and chaos."

I shrug.

"Honestly, it's not much different."

"Doesn't matter. We need to head the other way."

An alligator crawls out of a drain and begins chasing after a group of curly-haired women. I wonder what they did to deserve an eternity of this. One of them ends up caught and becomes intimate with the largest set of teeth I've ever laid eyes on.

"If we don't find Marcus soon, I'm going to have a breakdown. Either that or vomit."

Ash looks at me, then double takes when he seems to realize how deathly serious I am. He nods and turns back, leading me away from the alligator and towards an entrance to the subway station. We walk down the stairs, avoiding the grime-caked handrails and broken escalators.

"This is how demons and other low-level workers get around. I don't know whether or not they're after us, but I don't trust them. Keep quiet and follow me."

There's a surprising lack of giant animals down here, only the occasional person walking by; although, something about their bearing makes me think they may not be people at all.

"Okay," Ash says, flattening us against a disgusting wall.

"We need a disguise for you."

"You too," I point out. "Gerald Empusa targeted you. Neither of us is safe."

He nods, then removes his coat and drapes it over his head as if to protect himself from rain, before taking me by the shoulders and turning me to face the wall.

"Wait here," he says, and I hear him scamper away on bare feet. I hope that randomly facing walls is a more common occurrence down here, because this feels even more conspicuous than standing around, twiddling my thumbs.

Thankfully, he returns quickly.

"Do you still have your knife?" he asks.

I pull it out of my pocket and turn to him. He has the coat back on properly and a bright orange traffic cone in each hand.

"What are they for?" I ask, dreading the answer.

He doesn't respond, just sets them down, grabs the knife, and stabs one. He cuts out one hole, then two, and hands it to me. It takes me a second to register what he wants.

"Oh no," I tell him. "You cannot be serious." He continues holding it out, making puppy dog eyes. *Ugh.* I put the traffic cone on my head and realize that this is, without a doubt, the lowest point in my life so far. At least up until now, I felt sort of postapocalyptic in my bedraggled state, but this is ludicrous. The inside of the cone smells like old plastic and canola oil. What a combination.

Ash repeats the process on the second cone, hands the knife back to me, and sticks it over his own head. At least we're in this together. I take a long look at his eyes, peeking out from holes so lopsided they're almost triangular, and laugh. It is a long, wheezing, pained laugh that keeps going until I'm hunched over, holding the cone on with my hands.

"Oh god," I say, tears coming out of my eyes.

Ash gives a sympathetic giggle, and hearing it reverberate inside the cone makes me lose it again. I try to look him dead-on but can't keep myself upright and together.

"Are you alright, Jules?" he asks after I laugh for an uncomfortable amount of time, exhaling wheezes more than actual laughter.

"No, I think I've finally lost it. This is me officially going insane."

I double over again, the cracks in the tiled floor making me think of my own mental state right now.

"We should get moving."

He walks towards the entrance. I follow, barely stifling the crazy sounds coming out of my nose. Without any warning, he picks me up and half lifts, half tosses me over the metal bar of the turnstiles. I bang my knee against it and shout. It's a much louder sound than any of my recent experiences of having knives and needles shoved into me have elicited. I am no longer laughing.

"Shh."

Ash follows, the metal bars letting him walk through. *Show-off*. He points to a sign with an unfamiliar symbol on it. I figure it's the name of whichever subway line we need to get on considering how similar it looks to everything I saw while researching demonic sigils.

That was a different lifetime.

The two of us speed walk in the direction of the symbol, past the occasional winged beast with a mop bucket and posters advertising nonexistent television series. We head down a small set of stairs to a moderately packed platform. Across the tracks, on the opposite side, a woman with hair so long it hits the floor and circles around her feet plays a saxophone. "Careless Whisper." She's quite good. On our side stands a mess of failed experiments in creation, from what appears to be a human man with the neck of a giraffe—fur and all—to a group of elementary schoolers with transparent skin.

Also, a horse.

It takes a lot of willpower to not break and ask Ash for specifics on the demonic natures of everyone around us. What a wealth of insanity. Imagine writing it all down and turning it into a screenplay; Marcus would be on the short list to star in it, and what a fantastic avenue to use for us to fall in love. Except I don't need these fantasies anymore; I'm about to meet him in person quite soon. It hits me.

"Oh my god," I say, and Ash looks at me, startled. "What's wrong?"

"I'm about to meet Marcus K. Dixon."

"Shut. Up."

I assume Ash is glaring under his traffic cone, but I can't help it when a smile appears on my face. This vague plan of saving his life has existed for so long purely as a theoretical that

I never bothered to imagine how it would actually feel—not beyond fantasies that crumble in the sunlight.

A train barrels into the station, metal screeching against metal in a grotesque cacophony of city sounds. The doors open and we get on, Ash having to duck in order not to bash the traffic cone against the doorway, and we lean against the door on the opposite side of the car. Someone is performing a striptease around a metal pole farther down, and there's a robot reclined across three seats reading a newspaper. A voice over the speaker makes several announcements in a language I don't know. There's a little old lady with wriggling, forest green hair who is either staring at us or zoned out completely. After one stop, a mariachi band boards. After two, we've been asked for money by five homeless people. After the third stop, Ash nudges me and whispers.

"I don't think they're onto us, but keep your knife handy just in case. That lady is freaking me out."

It's hard to hear through all the layers of plastic and the general sound of public transportation. I give him a thumbs up directly in front of his eye holes, turning to do so.

His eyes go wide behind the plastic and suddenly I'm seeing much better.

The cone is gone.

I whip my head around and see that an old woman is holding it and staring at me with a manic grin on her face. There are a few moments of calm where we stare at one another, and then, almost as if it's been choreographed, everyone's heads snap up in unison and there are dozens of eyes on us. The stripper stops spinning around the pole and dangles upside down, looking our way with legs clamped tightly in place.

At least this is only a bunch of demons who may or may not want us dead and not something truly hellish like a flash mob. We brace ourselves for an attack; Ash gives up the pretense and throws his traffic cone to the side with a sharp intake of breath.

Nothing happens. They stare. The lady grins. The newspaper falls off the robot's lap, and no one even glances over when it hits the floor. I don't know if I reach for Ash or he reaches for me, but we hold hands and try to keep an eye on everyone in the car while also barely turning our heads.

The train slows. There are more words I don't understand. It jolts to a stop. Doors slide open and we rush out, only letting go of one another to navigate around the pole. Ash kicks a garbage bin over as we dash out of the station as if he hopes it will fend off anyone in pursuit; but, as it turns out, no one is in pursuit.

"Ash," I say. "We don't need to run. Look."

He glances over his shoulder and grinds to a halt on the platform.

"Oh."

The demons here are also staring, but no one actually does anything. I grasp the knife firmly in my hand and head to the stairs. When we get above ground, it's nighttime. Whether that's permanent or from the actual transition of day into night is anyone's guess. The area looks posh, with no building higher than five or six stories, and we're next to a small, grassy square with some white statues inside, glistening in nonexistent moonlight.

"Some celebrities end up farther downtown than this," Ash says, "in an area lovingly called 'business-district-on-the-weekends.' From what I've heard about it back in the diner, it's eerily empty and extremely claustrophobic. Perfect for the outgoing, self-absorbed, traditional celebrity personality type."

"It makes sense that Marcus isn't there. He's not self-absorbed at all."

"No, he's worse," Ash says grimly as we walk through the apocalyptic streets, grey and dangerous.

He stops at a door with an old, swinging sign hanging above it. It's blood red with the words *Marbas' Crisis* painted on it in flaking gold leaf.

"Welcome to your boy toy's personal Hell."

This is it. With all the staring and the panicking, I haven't had time to prepare. What will I say? Surely I've rehearsed some options, but I can't think of a single made-up conversation right now. My head is foggy. Dream-like. Ash leans against the door, holding it open for me—and I pause walking in.

"How do I look?" I ask.

"Seriously?"

"Yes."

"You're covered in blood, shirtless, and wrapped in enough bandages that you could use your arm as a pillow. You'll be the best-looking thing he's seen in ages."

"You say the sweetest things."

I head down the stairs. There's another door at the bottom, this one with a large window that allows me to see the desolation inside. From the looks of it, this place used to be a bar, but a tornado—or perhaps a toddler with chainsaw arms—has been through recently. The bronze doorknob is smooth and cool under my hand, and there's a gentle tinkling sound as I open the door. Step after step, I enter slowly, with Ash following close behind, pressed up against my back. The place is small, with only two tables and a piano standing between me and the bar that lines the back wall. Everything smells of cheap booze and stale air. The piano plays discordant notes at irregular intervals; no one presses the keys but sound comes out nonetheless. For the first time since I've entered Hell, I feel properly, nightmarishly creeped out.

"This place is scary," I whisper, continuing to step slowly.

"What did you expect?"

I pause at the piano and watch the keys move up and down. "Marcus is definitely in here?" I ask.

"He should be."

"Wait here, by the door," I tell Ash, and he nods in return.

It gives me courage. That's a lie—I pretend like it gives me courage, which is basically the same thing.

"Marcus K. Dixon," I shout, turning. "I'm here to rescue you!"

There's a noise behind the bar and my heart goes into overdrive; it just about disco dances out of my chest. My legs take me to the back of the room, but my insides feel like they stay right in the middle of the floor and fail to catch up. There's a chair on its side and I use it to climb on top of the bar and jump over, accidentally kicking and shattering a Jäger bottle in the process. Green glass everywhere.

I land directly on top of a body and realize, without a doubt, that it's a shape I know better than my own. My legs bracket a perfectly sized chest as hypnotic brown eyes stare up at me. Once my heart catches up to me, it falls right back out through my stomach.

"Marcus," I breathe.

"Hello," he says, and I internally have a few stern words with my body where I kindly inform it to not pass out or else there will be dire consequences. It is the body of a sophisticated, badass woman who absolutely fucking did it, not some weak collection of bones, flesh, and blood that flows in the wrong direction.

Breathe.

I stare into his eyes for what must be an uncomfortable amount of time, regardless of whether or not I'm the most beautiful thing he's seen in ages, then remember myself and move to stand on one side of him. The man can be trapped between my legs at a later date.

Look at me, one glance at him in the flesh and I've become a bad erotica writer. No wonder he's been the muse for so many soft-focus sex scenes. *Ha ha*, I think. *Who's into girls now?*

A voice in the back of my head says *You are*, but I push it away.

He moves to sit up, and I squat in front of him in the extremely limited space behind the bar.

"Who are you?" he asks, and I can die happy knowing that he has officially acknowledged my existence.

If this was on Earth, I would marvel over breathing his air. But I'm not certain if there's air down here. Or breathing.

"I'm here to help you, I'm—"

"Yes, but what's your name?"

His tone is frantic, which makes sense, and the accent is even more wonderful in person than I dared hope.

"Julia Tolliver."

"Julia. I've heard so much about you."

It's a strange thing for him to say, but then he smiles and my insides go all funny.

"Perfect."

He shoves a shard of glass deep into my chest.

CHAPTER ELEVEN

In which things end, but not really.

Dear Marcus,

I have this fantasy where you're nominated for an Oscar and I don't attend the ceremony with you because we got into a massive lovers' spat that morning. You win. Onstage, you cry and say how you don't deserve me but, regardless of that, you're selfish. You propose to me in front of the entire world, knowing full well that you're in the wrong. Luckily, I'm watching the Oscars at a nearby bar and sprint out the doors, run to the theater in a ball gown I was conveniently wearing, and announce proudly to security that I'm the woman who was just proposed to on national television and they'll let me through to see my fiancé or else.

The daydream typically goes a bit hazy around here but it's a nice one nonetheless.

Yours forever,
Julia R. Tolliver

If I were eloquent, I would say that being stabbed is the second most painful thing in the world, only beaten out by heartbreak. Except, of course, that's crap. Being stabbed is the most painful thing you can experience, period. Admittedly, I'm uncertain whether the tears are on account of the agony slicing through my chest or the complete betrayal. *What a shitty way to die.* Cool, but shitty, and completely unfair.

Shouting. Banging. Something is happening but there's no power that can get me to turn my head and look. It's just me and a dangling fluorescent light, yellow and swinging ever so slightly. *Is there a breeze in here? Funny.*

1, 2, 3, 4, 5, 6.

1, 2, 3, 4, 5, 6.

I set the swinging motion to a beat of six in my mind, like what I learned somewhere at some time, and blink slowly as it moves to the made-up rhythm in my head.

1, 2, 3, 4, 5, 6.

1, 2, 3, 4, 5, 6.

Everything makes sense. Hopefully all that screaming isn't coming from Ash. Time to close my eyes.

The sound goes away until there are only piano notes, poorly timed, and then an ocean takes up residence between my eardrums. Swishing and splashing and . . .

> *Jules finds out in fourth period. Why do all the worst things happen in science class? After finishing the quiz early—not because she was particularly good, but because she knew so few answers—she pulls out her phone to check Marcaddicts, the blog of a young woman who stalks the sets of Marcus K. Dixon films and posts photos online with theories about what's happening in the plotlines. Jules looks at this blog at least once every forty minutes, when she's walking from one class to another, but sometimes more frequently. Like right now, when she deserves a reward after a crappy quiz.*

The first post is not a photo, which is strange. It's two words.

Kill me.

Jules feels as if she's having an out-of-body experience as she continues scrolling and sees a reposted news article from the BBC.

Marcus K. Dixon is dead. Dead.

Her arms are not her arms. Her body is not her body.

Jules drops her phone and everyone looks at her. Without grabbing a hall pass, without telling the teacher anything, she runs to the bathroom and vomits violently. It's disgusting. She barely remembers the inconsolable weeping, being nearly dragged out of the bathroom, being asked if she was on drugs. If she was suicidal.

Her parents are unable to see reason. They don't understand why she had to leave school early just because an actor died. This is not simply an actor dying, though. Teenagers need a life raft, something to get them through how awful it is to exist. It used to be religion, but now it's boy bands. Television shows. British actors. What reason does Jules have to wake up, to go to school anymore? She used to go "life sucks, but at least Marcus is happy and one day there'll be a new Fletcher Fatale film." Now there's no bright point in the future to survive until.

There's no future where she marries Marcus. There isn't even the wonderful fantasy of it to get her through sleepless nights.

She understands Marcaddicts completely.

"Kill me," she whispers into her pillow at night. "It's so lonely in my head without him."

Piano notes. There are discordant piano notes filling the air, and pain filling my chest. I didn't die. *Huh.*

I mean, not that I was particularly looking forward to the whole death thing, but it does seem like a bit of a departure from the typical result of getting stabbed in the chest. It still hurts unlike anything I've ever experienced before, but that's it.

Eyes open. I sit up. My bra is soaked in blood. I use one arm to lean against the shelves beneath the bar and the other to hold my head.

"Ouch," I announce in a glorious understatement.

Someone must hear me, judging by the immediate banging from the other side of the bar.

"Jules? What the fuck?"

"Oh, hey Ash. Think you can help me out with . . ." I gesture limply in the general vicinity of my chest.

He continues to be fantastically unhelpful, though, and leans over the bar to stare down at me, looking considerably more banged up than before.

"That didn't kill you?"

"Apparently not."

"There's no way that couldn't have killed you."

I shrug. There being no way for something to be possible doesn't stop it from being true.

Otherwise, how would bees fly? I'm not making sense, but that should be allowed. I was just stabbed, after all. Ash clambers over the bar, crouches down in front of me, places a hand on my cheek, then yanks the glass out of my chest without warning.

"Ouch," I say yet again, this time with much more pomp. Aren't you not supposed to touch stabby things lodged in your body? Something about bleeding out. Not that it matters much anymore.

Ash appears to realize something, and I mentally brace myself because there's no way it's going to be good. He stares into my eyes and takes a deep breath, obviously working himself up to say whatever the bad news is.

"I thought this might have happened, but I guess it was easier to not think about it too much."

"You knew that Marcus would try to kill me? You bastard."

That genuinely does piss me off. Ash and I had finally formed a sort of alliance, and he let me walk straight into that mess? Not cool.

"No. Not that. This didn't kill you," he throws the shard of glass across the floor, "because you're already dead."

"*I'm sorry, what?*" I screech, like a middle-aged woman who wants to speak to the manager.

"Here, let me help you up."

He reaches for me, but I bat away his hand and press myself into the bar.

"No. Absolutely not. What do you mean I'm already dead?"

Ash looks wrecked and is once again working himself up to answer when a tinkling sound rings out from the doorway.

"It means that someone's destiny, no matter how unstable, cannot be altered," comes a woman's voice.

I pull myself up, ignoring Ash's offer to help me stand, and see three women on the opposite end of the room, standing directly in front of the doorway like they're posing for some sort of movie poster.

"Or, more precisely," the same voice continues, and I see it belongs to the woman standing in the center, "it means that we won."

She holds out both hands and the women standing on either side high-five her without looking. *Neat.* Except the last time I saw the other two, one had a pair of scissors protruding from her neck and the other was absolutely massive and doing her best to step on me. The Fates.

"Hello, shrew," Ash says, his voice coming from behind me.

The woman speaking nods her head and I realize she must be the first Fate he met, the one who owned the scissors.

The one-eyed shrew who does nothing but sit on her ass and snip the intellectual golden threads of the craftsman's loom.

The size of her posterior certainly implies she's the one who does nothing but sit, that's for certain. In other circumstances, I might even be a bit jealous. They all take a step forward in unison, a rather large one, and I realize that's to get over an extremely battered-looking Marcus K. Dixon, who's curled up in the middle of the floor. I feel something but don't know what it is. Something that sits in my chest, behind the wound, and doesn't move.

"Am I really dead?" I ask, my voice coming out all wrong.

"Yes. Valac killed you back in Saint Abaddon Hospital. Evidently the message that he succeeded never got to Marcus, though. He hasn't been the most perceptive. Pity." She doesn't sound surprised at all.

"You wanted me dead. You wanted them all to kill me. Over some stupid scissors and some stupid flash drive? You—"

I go to leap over the bar, not sure what I'm going to do once I get my hands on them, but certain it'll be nasty. Ash holds me back.

"We are The Fates," the woman on the left states. "But, more importantly, we are your fate."

"You have never had any control," the one all the way on the right continues in the same tone and voice. "Not on Earth and certainly not here. What we want hardly matters, but what you want is beyond insignificant."

"This was all with good reason," the middle Fate says, with a certain earnestness I didn't get from the others. "Losing one's life is much more preferable to losing one's death, which is exactly what you have been attempting to do to someone else. There are significantly worse outcomes than this for a mortal woman."

I'm shaking. If I'm dead, how can I be shaking? That's so human, to tremble with fright. "How did I not notice I died?" I collapse against Ash, who helps me stay somewhat upright. I'm not looking at him, or Marcus, or The Fates. Just my hands. They look the same as they always have.

"Because you ended up where you were always meant to end up. I know all the questions you want to ask. Yes, Marcus is a monster and yes, we put him up to this. He was only an insurance plan, though, so his failure is not too great of a shock."

One of them nudges Marcus' leg with her foot and he lets out a groan, barely audible.

They take another step forward.

"Yes, we let you escape from Drizzlyland. To think we would not follow you was an idiot's dream. Specifically, the dream of the idiot standing behind you."

Another step.

"Yes, you had to die, but it was not without good cause. We have a mission for you."

"I don't want your mission. I want to go back home."

I'm crying, not that I do much else anymore. I cry for my college education, and my parents, and Laura, but mainly for myself.

"This is your home."

They reach me. The Fate standing in the middle places both hands on the counter and leans forward, filling my vision completely. A smile, full of pointed wooden teeth.

"Welcome to Hell. We won't hurt you any more than necessary. We need you too much for that."

Ash yanks me back, and I'm truly starting to get sick of everyone moving me around however they please. He loops one arm around my shoulders and uses his free hand to lift up a section of the bar for us to walk through.

"Come on, Jules. We'll figure this all out," he whispers, trying to get me past the three women even though they take up nearly the entire width of the room.

I think about my "condition," which Gerald Empusa had referred to. How everyone on the subway knew we were odd but not worth attacking. How had word spread so fast? How had I not known?

I was already dead when I met Faith.

"No. I have more questions. This can't be true. This all," I flail my arms wildly, "can't be true. Marcus isn't evil, he didn't try to kill me, Ash didn't beat him up, and I haven't been dead for God knows how long!"

"He doesn't," says the Fate closest to me.

"What?"

"God doesn't know how long you've been dead for. I doubt he

even knows you're in Hell. Why stop there? I almost guarantee you that God doesn't even know you were born to begin with."

"I don't believe in God!"

"He doesn't believe in you either," she shoots back. "But we do. Go. Let your cute friend with the awful ideas take you away. You'll find we're not nearly as bad as you think."

"You had me killed."

"Semantics. Everyone dies. There's some bribery waiting outside for you."

"That's it? You just show up and explain everything and send me on my merry way?" This is all too much. My brain feels like it's about to melt and drip straight out of my ears, but I might not even have a brain anymore. Who knows what you have when you don't have a life.

"Think of it as a *deus ex machina*, just in case you decide to turn this into a play eventually. We have our reasons, and very soon, you'll have yours as well."

Ash nudges me forward and this time, I go willingly. I still feel ghostly and out of it, which actually makes sense, in a sick kind of way. The proper breakdown will arrive any second and it's better to have more space when it really hits.

I step over Marcus' body, saving that moment to process later. The door tinkles as we exit. Five steps to street level. Another door. My car is inexplicably parked in front of Marbas' Crisis. I walk to it silently and enter. Ash gets into the other side. There's a note on the steering wheel that says "Open the Glove Compartment," which I wordlessly pass to Ash, continuing to stare straight out the windshield at the city. Death is not as empty as I would have thought. I hear a click and a rustle.

"Julia Rosenthal Tolliver," he reads. Hearing my full name in his voice, not in some unwilling memory, nearly breaks me. But not yet. "You do not belong here. Not as a human and not now that you are dead. This is wrong. We do not belong here, either. The Fates once ruled in Heaven and we will again. We know you can argue. We have seen those books you've read on the law. Prepare your defense and sue God for your place in Heaven. Ash can help, as he once lived there and has the means to contact them, whether he knows it or not."

Ash's voice shakes. He clears his throat and carries on.

"It will be tempting to not do as we ask, but you know we are correct and you will help us begin a revolution. This is not Armageddon. This is what is correct. Remember that we can see you at all moments."

"They must have written that note before I handed Faith over to Otis if they think I don't belong here," I say.

We're both silent. "Jules, what do you—"

"I'm going to turn on this car and drive."

"And then what?"

"And then I'm going to drive some more. I may stop and scream for a bit, but let's get out of here first."

"Are you going to sue God for The Fates?"

As I turn on the car, my brain is awash with arguments. Ones I used against people who thought it was perverse that I believed Fletcher Fatale and Ferdinand Ferdinand belonged together. In-depth analyses on morality and theology and fan culture.

Arguments that a group of mythical creatures apparently want me to use against the creator of everything.

But that's for later. It has to be.

I take a deep breath, turn to Ash, and smile so wide my cheeks ache. It's a happy burn.

"First things first. There's a beautiful girl who I promised to save from a horrible old demon. I'm going to go and get her. We'll figure out everything else after that."

He returns the smile, slowly, and then with a great tidal wave of feeling and unspoken conversations. "Sounds like a plan," he says. "Let's drive."

And we do.

ABOUT THE AUTHOR

Calista Lynne is a novelist and theatre-maker currently based in New York City. She can usually be found drinking coffee and wearing pink. Other works by her include *We Awaken*, published in 2016.

E-mail: officialcalista@gmail.com

ACKNOWLEDGMENTS

This book would be nothing without my lovely beta readers: Alexander R. Polt-Gifford, Aubrey Urbach, Emily, Ira, Noama, Paula Aguirre, and Sara Hamraz. I know people say too many cooks is a bad thing, but you all made the dish that much sweeter.

My friends are my world. Tania has a name that anagrams so perfectly into Anita. Kait ran away with me during a pandemic and wrote fanfiction as I wrote this book. So many others have given me so much.

I must thank my parents—who are the greatest a queer girl could ask for—as well as the entire LGBTQ community. You are all my family.

This book is a love letter to every owner and operator of a roadside attraction. You made moving back to America much less painful.

And, finally, thank you to Benedict Cumberbatch. When I was a teenager, I would have walked straight into Hell for you, and now I don't even know what movies you've been in for the past six years. Growing up is truly something else.

Amble Press, an imprint of Bywater Books, publishes fiction and narrative nonfiction by LGBTQ writers, with a primary, though not exclusive, focus on LGBTQ writers of color. For more information on our titles, authors, and mission, please visit our website.

www.amblepressbooks.com

www.ingramcontent.com/pod-product-compliance
Lightning Source LLC
Chambersburg PA
CBHW050402110726
47899CB00008B/2615